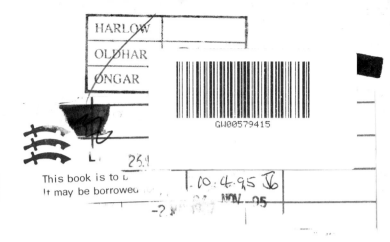

THE WEB

The Web

Henri Troyat

Translated from the French by
Anthea Bell

AIDAN ELLIS

First published in the United Kingdom by Aidan Ellis
Publishing Ltd., Cobb House, Nuffield, Henley-on-Thames,
Oxon RG9 5RU

English translation copyright © 1984 by Aidan Ellis

Originally published in French, L'araigne, copyright
© Librairie Plon 1938

First edition 1984

Printed and bound in Great Britain by Redwood Burn Limited,
Trowbridge, Wiltshire.
Photoset in Great Britain by Carlton Photosetters,
Westcliff-on-Sea, Essex.

British Library Cataloguing in Publication Data:

Troyat, Henri
  The Web
  Rn. Lev Terrason   I. Title   II. L'araigne
  English
  843'.914(F)   PQ2639.R78

ISBN 0 85628 131 X

PART 1

I

The doorbell rang, startling him. He looked at his watch: one o'clock. Neither his mother nor his sisters could be back yet. There were footsteps coming down the echoing corridor. Gérard Fonsèque sat up in bed.

"Who's that?"

"Me, Lequesne. Am I disturbing you?"

The door opened. A tall young man stood there; his face was brown and hard as flint, his eyes sultry like a girl's. His Adam's apple protruded distinctly from a neck inflamed by the razor. He wore patent leather shoes.

He stopped in the bedroom doorway, taken aback. The half-closed shutters kept the atmosphere of the room dim, warm and hazy. Shelves crammed with books were fixed to the walls. Papers spread over the table, surrounding a plaster skull which was really an inkwell. There was a smell of acrid perspiration and medicaments in the air.

Lequesne went over to the bed where his friend lay, unshaven and unwell, sweating feverishly, and shook his damp hand.

"Fled from the nuptial rejoicings, have you?" inquired Gérard.

"Your mother said you were ill. I wanted to come and see you. How are you feeling?"

"Better, thanks. So how was the ceremony? Tedious, I suppose?"

"No, it all went very well."

"Yes, that's what I meant!"

Fonsèque laughed, rubbing the burning palms of his limp hands together. He had not wanted to attend his sister's wedding, and two days beforehand he had gone out walking in the rain without a hat or coat, with the valiant intention of catching cold. At the moment his temperature must be well above normal, but what would he not have borne to spare himself the sight of Luce coming into church, walking up the aisle, kneeling beside that fellow Paul Aucoc, pallid and plump like a scavenging cat? "Can't stand all that religious pomp and ceremony!" he muttered. "Such a display of clothes and fuss and gossip! It's the shabbily theatrical side of it all that disgusts me—the paper frills round the smoked ham! All right, let's have the details! How did Luce look?"

"Beautiful. Radiant and self-possessed."

"That's compulsory. Tradition says so!"

"When she came in on your uncle's arm . . ." Lequesne was speaking slowly, as if he either had to pick his words, or was reluctant to recall the scene. Gérard listened with strained attention. Every word drove home that sense of pain and suppressed fury which had been afflicting him for weeks, yet he was avid to hear more.

"Were there many people there?"

"Yes, it took the procession ages to get into the sacristy."

Gérard immediately conjured up a picture of the cramped sacristy, with the young couple and their families lined up against the wall as if facing a firing squad, saw the guests marking time as they slowly advanced, the congratulations and embraces as Luce and Paul Aucoc introduced their friends to each other. "My husband . . . my wife." Sharing everything already—their first household chattels!

"Who did you notice?"

"Er . . . Madame Rouget. The Chaumonts. Monsieur Duplessis, Monsieur Garde . . ."

All those worn faces! Every last one of their acquaintances had been invited. A full house, every seat booked! What a farce it was!

"Did you hear any comments?"

"Well, yes, of course—very flattering ones."

Yes, such as: "There's one man with a good time ahead of him tonight!" That was the kind of flattering comment usually made in the circumstances. Oh, it was a good marriage; Paul was an excellent catch. M. Aucoc senior owned a salted provisions factory, and his son worked in the business with him. But it wasn't the man himself Luce loved. She was marrying him for a fine apartment, for his business connections, for holidays in the South of France. She had siezed her chance with the haste of any ambitious little tart; with the rapacious, petty greed of those women who pounce upon the displays of goods in big stores, rummaging through piles of remnants, jostling and clawing each other to get the best bit in their trembling hands. Luce had got the best bit. She was happy. Her mother was happy. Everybody was happy, except Gérard.

He remembered Mme Fonsèque's face, beaming with mercenary satisfaction, on the morning when she told him the news. "Luce is engaged." He had not realized the full extent of the catastrophe straight away. It was over the next few days that his fearful sufferings began. Luce was no longer herself. She had left the fashion house where she had been working for the last two years; she and her mother talked of nothing but clothes and furniture, guest lists and precedence. As the day came closer, the two families visted each other with increasing, indeed excessive frequency. The Aucocs came to see the Fonsèques. The Fonsèques went to see the Aucocs. The two clans were being merged. The soft domestic cocoon was in preparation. There were interminable dinners at which M. Aucoc senior, a corseted giant of a man with heavy jowls and a dyed moustache, made speeches in his deep voice, and everyone had to wait for him to finish before the plates could be changed. Coffee was taken in the drawing room, with Luce and Paul playing the parts of exemplary turtle doves, sitting hand in hand and gazing into each other's eyes. Sometimes Luce's fiancé would show photographs, and Luce herself went into ecstasies over them, squealing girlishly, "Goodness, is it really you on the rock? How funny! Oh, look, isn't that one funny too? And that one—oh, that one's a scream!"

When the Aucocs had left, she would pick up a sketch pad and design initials to go on her trousseau. One evening she handed Gérard several sheets of paper covered with circles, squares, diamond shapes, all with the letters L.F.A. lovingly entwined in their centres.

"Give me your advice, will you?"

But the monograms, with their interlacing lines, evoked so clear an idea of the couple's union that he did not know what to say. He felt stunned and sad to the point of tears. He must talk about something else, quick. Say something, anything.

"Well, never mind all that. The family will tell me all about the wedding this evening, and I mustn't spoil their fun."

He was panting slightly. He glanced surreptitiously at Lequesne, and saw that the young man looked tired and abstracted. He was skimming through the translation lying on the table; it was of an English detective story, and Gérard had been working on it for the last few days.

"I haven't got much further," Gérard said. "The publisher's in a hurry, but that's just too bad. I'm putting my mind to my philosophical essay on Evil."

"You haven't given that idea up, then?"

"No, why should I? It'll be an essential standard work—for myself as well as other people! A marvellous pair of glasses through which to view the Universe! The message of Scripture is confused, dated. There are a couple of lines by de Vigny that sum the whole thing up perfectly:

When gods come down upon the worlds, they find
The tracks are deep that they must leave behind.

"So where are those deep tracks? Where are the furrows they've ploughed for us—tracks along which we can start without fear of coming to a dead end, or getting trapped? Wherever I may be, and in whatever circumstances, I am alone. In short, there's no one to pray to but myself. I've learnt in a hard school—but I've acquired a certain practised lucidity there. I'm proud of that, and I'd like others to profit by it too. What a fine saying that is of Nietzsche's, that 'Man is something to be overcome'! The *Über-Ich*! It would make a splendid epigraph for my essay, wouldn't it? What do you think?"

12

"No, I don't agree. We are never forgotten and never free!"

"A Jansenist, are you?"

"I wouldn't like you to think I pride myself on the kind of fatalism which simply says everything's predestined, Fonsèque, and we can't alter our actions in the least particular. I'd call that sheer cowardice. What I believe is something different. How can I make you understand? Look, have you ever played tennis, been to a tennis tournament? Sorry about using such a sporting metaphor, but think of a doubles match. One of your opponents sends the ball back. It comes over the net. Even before it touches the ground you can tell, just from the way it's travelling, if it's going to be your ball or if you'd do better to leave it to your partner. It all depends on the trained eye. Well, the same applies to life. When I find myself facing some dilemma, a curious intuition gives me information about it, and then I know, directly, if it's up to me to act or if I should leave it to my partner. Because he's there all right, behind me, my invisible, watchful and powerful partner, and if I poach when the ball's in his court I may lose the point! You're smiling, Fonsèque, you think it's a puerile theory—"

"No, not at all. But if you won't intervene in the course of your own life then you must, *a fortiori*, renounce all right to comment on anyone else's, mustn't you?"

"Yes, of course."

"So if you saw your best friend was about to take an unwise decision, you ought not even to acknowledge that you might be able to prevent him?"

"No."

"But that's ridiculous!" cried Fonsèque. "Listen, you'd help a blind man over the road! So why not help somebody blinded by passion? That's just as real a form of blindness."

"Because you can't tell which of the pair of you really *is* blind."

"Oh, come on! I've thought about such things too much and worked on them too hard not to be able to see what way people should go, what dangers they ought to avoid, what pleasures they should choose!"

13

"Then why can't you apply all that discernment to your own life?"

"I'm happy!"

"No, Fonsèque, you are not." Lequesne shook his head slightly. The dim light in the room made his face look flat, like a mask, with deep-set, shadowed eyes and pitch-black hair. His arms were folded over his chest.

"I'll study the question in my essay," said Gérard. "For a start, your attitude suggests that of the established mystics. As St Chantal wrote, 'I need do nothing but leave God to act.'"

Lequesne shrugged his shoulders, and did not reply. Gérard looked at him in some surprise.

"I say, is this discussion boring you?"

"No, I'm just surprised you can talk philosophy on a day like this."

"Perhaps it's only to avoid talking about other things!"

Gérard instantly regretted making this remark, but Lequesne did not seem to have understood him. He was looking down at his hands. Gérard heard him breathing hard, as if he had been wringing something in his long, thin fingers. What lay behind his melancholy attitude? Gérard had always suspected his friend of having a fondness for Luce, but was it to be supposed he was so much in love with her as to feel pain at her marriage? Could he, Gérard, have been so completely wrong about him? There was that silence, that rapid breathing, those drooping shoulders . . . yes, he had no doubt of it now! And he felt a certain vicious pleasure. There was someone to share his own distress at last. He did not feel sorry for Lequesne. (Had anyone felt sorry for *him*?) He wanted to hurt the silent, injured man, feast upon his cries of pain, forget his own unhappiness in watching the unhappiness he could cause.

"You're quite right," he said. "Philosophical conversations are all wrong on a wedding day. 'Alas for the spiritual poverty of a shared life! Alas for the wretchedness of a shared contentment!' Let's talk about Luce, then. What's your opinion of her?"

Lequesne jumped. "My opinion? I hardly knew her!"

14

"No, so you didn't. I'm really sorry about that. She was such an adorable girl—light-hearted, frank, childlike! You know, she came to see me before she left for church, looking lovelier than ever in her white dress."

As he spoke, Gérard was watching Lequesne. The lower he pitched his voice, the better he could appreciate the pain it was inflicting. There was a singular pleasure in seeing the young man at his mercy, unable to defend himself, solely concerned to master his emotions.

"A pity she's fallen into that oaf's hands. She deserved better. But there—she couldn't wait."

He had said such things to himself so often, it seemed quite strange to be repeating them to someone else. He went on, with deliberate malice.

"And where is she now? Off on her ridiculous honeymoon! Sitting in a railway carriage opposite her plump if elegant husband! They're talking confidentially through the noise of the wheels, without a thought for us, sitting here thinking of them . . ."

Lequesne had got out a cigarette, and was lighting it, with nervous movements.

"Please! Take pity on my poor throat!" said Gérard.

The young man stubbed his cigarette out in an ashtray, turned and went over to the window with its half-open shutters. A fine, fast rain was falling. The deserted Place des Vosges, with its stunted trees, pink stone façades and dark arcades, looked like some forlorn provincial avenue. A woman was slapping her doormat against one of the columns.

Lequesne came back to the foot of the bed. He looked exhausted, and his eyelids, with their long, feminine lashes, were blinking rapidly. His Adam's apple was going up and down his thin neck, as if he had been holding back tears.

"Were you in love with her?" Fonsèque suddenly asked.

Lequesne waited a moment, and then said, "Yes."

He had spoken calmly; he made no movement, did not even bend his head. Taken aback, Fonsèque let a few seconds go by.

15

Then he asked another question.

"And now you're upset?"

"Yes."

"You don't regret not trying to stop her marrying Aucoc?"

"What use would that have been?"

Fonsèque burst out laughing. "I suppose it wasn't the right moment? The ball was in your partner's court?"

"Yes, I think so."

"Honestly, my poor fellow, you should be put away!" He felt a sudden surge of hatred for his friend, as if he were to be blamed for Luce's marriage, and said brutally, "Well, there's nothing you can do about it now but get out of her life!"

"I never did occupy much space in it."

"How do you know?"

That was a good thrust! He must sow seeds of doubt, arouse compunction.

Lequesne looked up. His lashes were rather close together, his lower lip trembled slightly. "Look, let's not discuss this any more, all right?" he said faintly. "Never again . . . or not today, anyway."

*   *   *

Mme Fonsèque did not come home until half past seven. Lequesne had just left. She immediately began fussing about, seeing that Gérard had a cup of light broth, some rusks and some stewed fruit. She sat down beside him to tell him about the wedding, but he stopped her, saying he'd heard all the details from Lequesne, and as he was rather tired he would prefer her to keep quiet. Why wasn't she having any dinner herself?

"Oh, I'm not hungry. I did very well at the wedding breakfast!"

He thought the expression a ghastly one. She was still wearing her blue, watered satin dress. It made her look enormous and shiny, like a live lobster. Her grey hair was elaborately curled round her temples. Her pale, heavy cheeks

16

drooped, and the bags under her eyes had tiny wrinkles in them, like burst blisters. She seemed to be in an emotional, uneasy mood, at a loose end, and she was sniffing at frequent intervals.

Other evenings flashed through Gérard's mind: family evenings spent at his bedside. (Any little cold in the head was a good excuse for these gatherings.) His three sisters and his mother would come to his room to have their coffee, sitting round his bed. He saw his eldest sister Elisabeth's pale, firm, Roman face; the imperfect little profile of Marie-Claude, the youngest; Luce's painted, smiling mouth, her sensuous stretching, her soft yawns. They had been out and about in Paris all afternoon, rubbing shoulders with strangers, occupying themselves in a variety of ways—and then they returned to him, submissive, charming, full of mystery. And he kept them there, closed in the confinement of his room, safe from strange glances, merely by exercising the magic of his affection. This was their home port. There were private jokes, odd customs which he treasured all the more because an outsider would certainly have thought them absurd. They gave friends of the family silly nicknames. Julien Lequesne had been christened "Princess Juliana"; Vigneral was known as "Vineleaf". They awarded marks to everyone they knew.

"How many would you give Hurault?"

"Oh, seventeen out of twenty. He's doing better since he shaved his moustache off!"

Sometimes Marie-Claude and Luce exchanged frocks. It was delightful to see them come into the room dressed up as each other. He suddenly remembered the first time Luce went out in the evening, the first time she wore make-up. When she came home from the dance she had not wanted to take it off before she went to bed. He recalled her painted little urchin face, lips red as raw meat, eyes shining. He saw her looking into space, happy and a little intoxicated. She would look like that when she got into the big bed waiting for her this evening. She would leave her painted, decked-out, decorated face unwashed, the better to seduce the poor, fat, clumsy male who would come

17

across the room to get his ration of pleasure served up to him in the bed, as if in a manger.

Gérard shook his head and closed his eyes, revolted. This marriage was the ruin of all his illusions. He had wanted Luce's marriage to be something full of intelligence and grace. Now, the magnificent, mysterious husband of whom he had dreamed had dwindled to no more than Paul Aucoc, shapeless, flabby, and soft as a slug. What a gulf fixed between the marriage he had hoped for and the vile bargain she had struck today! Oh, the sadness of this lamentable bartering of bodies and self-interest, the humiliation of those amorous expressions attendant upon a manoeuvre from which love was surely excluded! But the union would gradually be cemented by the paltry acquiescence of the flesh. They would be a couple like other couples. A well-respected couple. And who knew—there might even be nights when they thought themselves happy!

Gently, Mme Fonsèque laid a hand on her son's forehead. "Your temperature's gone down," she said. "Luce was so sorry not to have you there!"

He gave a short laugh. "Oh, come! I could hardly be occupying her mind entirely on such a day!"

"No, of course not! But I remember, on my own wedding day . . ."

Why must mothers be so determined to discuss their own wedding days on the occasion of their daughters' marriages? He interrupted her.

"Where are Marie-Claude and Elisabeth?"

"Out at the theatre, with Paul's two best men. Oh, by the way, who do you think I saw in the sacristy? Joseph Tellier!"

She immediately regretted these words. Gérard had suddenly flushed red. "What's *he* after now?" he growled.

"Why, nothing, dear! Elisabeth may have turned him down, but that doesn't mean he mustn't have anything to do with us. He's a very nice person, a family friend as well as manager of our little shop."

"Which is losing you all you've got left!"

"That's not his fault. Between you and me, I'm rather sorry

18

your sister decided against him. Joseph Tellier would have been a very decent sort of catch for a girl of twenty-nine with as little money of her own as Elisabeth."

"What—a fellow of over forty, uneducated, without means or prospects, and crippled too? You think a lot of your daughter's interests, I must say!"

"Gérard, if you hadn't lectured her—"

"I didn't lecture her. I simply opened her eyes for her. She was fully aware of what she was doing when she made her choice, and I'm glad of it."

His voice was shaking, his eyes bright with fever. He wiped his face with a cloth hanging at the foot of the bed, and then fell back on his pillows. Mme Fonsèque did not like arguing with her son. She was afraid of him: he was so clever, so self-willed, so sensitive.

"Well, that's all old history now," she said. "Don't let's discuss it! How are you feeling?"

He did not reply. He was breathing hard, as if he had been in a fight. The greenish light shed by his reading lamp made his face look set and ill. The poor woman was alarmed. "Better take your temperature."

"No, no! Leave me alone!"

She got up and went out; she was going to tidy up in Luce's room. Gérard could hear her footsteps the other side of the wall between the two bedrooms, the squeak of drawers being opened, and now and then the sigh of a heavily built person bending to pick something up. A little later he thought he heard sobs. Why was she crying? Tears for a daughter whom she had flung into Aucoc's arms, into his bed? It was grotesque! Still, she liked weeping and moaning, poor thing. Ever since her husband's death she had lived in the expectation of some imminent disaster, and as she had four children she seemed to herself to have four times as many chances of unhappiness. How terrified she had been, three years ago, in case the Army Medical Board passed Gérard as fit for military service. However, they had rejected him as being of inadequate physique, which was both lucky and insulting.

At ten o'clock, Mme Fonsèque left the room next door, and Gérard heard her heavy steps retreating down the corridor. Now he was quite alone.

Alone until morning.

Elisabeth and Marie-Claude were out at the theatre with the best men. The young men would be wearing scraps of Luce's torn, dishonoured veil in their buttonholes. He remembered who they were: Hurault and Vigneral. He found Vigneral, who had been at school with him, exasperating. He was a strong young man with a red neck, a firm jaw, and the mind of a commercial traveller, which was indeed his profession. He seemed to be forever just getting out of some girl's bed, ready to be off in search of another adventure; his life was one of amorous campaigning—seductions, quarrels, reconciliations. It was hard to imagine anything but a woman making him either happy or unhappy. He patronized Gérard, and had been known to say, "Talking to you about mistresses is like you talking to me about literature—we're just not on the same wavelength!"

What a fool! One did not condemn the fleeting world of the senses outright; one set limits to it. One did not deny one's baser appetites; one subordinated them to an ideal conception of the world. One did not choose between the flesh and the spirit; one balanced those two opposing impulses, trying not to set the waterline too low!

I can see what they all really need better than they do, thought Gérard.

He was proud of being able to overcome material temptations himself. All that mattered was the inner life, the enrichment of the ego by reading, thinking and studying. One rose above the rough and tumble, one stood apart from the passions. Wasn't it better to keep out of a fight in order to understand its various phases? He derived strength from his isolation. Clearly and calmly, he foresaw what others, preoccupied with their petty struggles, would never notice until it was too late. As for Elisabeth and Tellier, well, he had saved her from a stultifying, shabby sort of life lived behind the shop,

20

with not much money and many business worries. He had saved her from herself and everyone else. She was grateful to him, too!

A sense of his own power swept over him, like an overwhelming yet tranquil ecstasy.

He closed his eyes and tried to sleep, but sleep would not come. Elisabeth and Marie-Claude aren't in yet, he thought, the're out enjoying themselves . . .

At two o'clock, he heard a key fumbling in the lock, and the voices of his two sisters talking to each other in the hall.

He switched off his light.

II

"Italy's the most beautiful country in the world. Paul adores me! I adore Paul! I'm out of my mind with joy! Kisses, kisses, kisses! Luce."

Mme Fonsèque smiled, beaming indulgently, and put the postcard down beside her plate.

"I'm sure the postman enjoyed that!" said Gérard. "Really, she might have sent us her purple prose under plain cover!"

"I think it's a very nice card," said Mme Fonsèque.

"You just can't understand, can you?"

"I can understand that my daughter's happy, dear, and that's enough for me."

Gérard put his napkin to his mouth, to stifle laughter. "That's really priceless! Being married has made the girl a perfect idiot, and you don't even mind?"

"Young married people who admit they're in love always seem a little comic to their friends," said Marie-Claude, with an air of wisdom.

"Well, thank you so much for giving us the benefit of your entire seventeen years' experience, my dear, but if you ask me they're going too far, even for young married people. Luce is a different person these days! She's made herself a fool in her husband's image—very generous of her! I expect she'll be speaking through her nose like Paul too by the time they come back from their honeymoon!"

"Oh, Gérard!"

Much pleased with his witticism, he stroked his jaw with his long, limp, well-manicured hand, and glanced at Elisabeth and Marie-Claude, as if to solicit their approval. Then he began toying with his meat again. It lay on his plate, surrounded by cold sauce. He was not hungry, he never was, but he liked mealtimes because they reunited his sisters and mother together around the old table. The ceiling lamp, made in the

22

form of a chandelier, the Henri II sideboard with its carved panels, the single window, its lower half clear, its upper half covered with cellophane in imitation of leaded stained glass, in lozenges of red and blue, all added up to an unchanging setting, and here the clan had re-grouped as best it might after Luce's departure. There was one less place laid at the table now, one face less, one voice less. Nothing would fill the void she had left: Luce with her painted face, her almost indecent abundance of red hair, her squirrel-like little ways.

She would murmur remarks such as, "I've decided to alter my evening dress—I'm going to give it a coiled belt: white Italian crêpe and Chartreuse green uncrushable velvet."

"A coiled belt will make your waist look thicker," said Marie-Claude.

"No, it won't, not if the fabric's cut on the bias."

"It'll make you look like a frontier post, then!"

Once upon a time, these trivial discussions had annoyed Gérard. Now he actually missed the sharp exasperation he used to feel at the sight and sound of Luce, his desire to tell her in detail how silly she was and then make a loving apology later. On the other hand, it struck him that he dominated his now smaller family more easily. It was as if Luce's marriage had drawn his mother and his two remaining sisters closer to him, delivering them up to him even more trusting than before. He felt a constant urge to try out his power over them.

"I've often thought about the mimesis of married women," he remarked. "Isn't it odd to see how few of them manage to preserve their own personalities? As Nietzsche said: 'A man's happiness is *I want*, a woman's happiness is *he wants*.'"

Elisabeth had stopped eating. Perhaps she realised he was really talking to her. He wanted to remind her that he admired her for refusing Tellier's proposal of marriage, for her cold, virginal pride and her intelligence. She must be happy, and she must know it: that mattered. But Elisabeth did not let her feelings show. She was reserved, enigmatic, hard to approach. He went on, however.

"And indeed, I wonder if married women even realize what

they've lost? Most of them just strip themselves of individuality straight away, neutralize themselves, flatten themselves out, fit into their husbands' exact mould. 'Italy's the most beautiful country in the world. Paul adores me! I adore Paul! I'm out of my mind with joy!' Hm . . . no comment!"

"Well, you're certainly giving me some interesting insights into the masculine mentality," said Marie-Claude, and immediately blushed. Gérard burst out laughing.

"My dear, your conversation is absolutely scintillating!"

"What have I said that's so funny? I don't see it!"

"Never mind, you can leave that to other people!"

"Oh, children, children!" wailed Mme Fonsèque.

Gérard mopped his face with his handkerchief. He enjoyed such skirmishes, seeking out occasions for them with avidity and patience, and then relishing them, head thrown back, lower lip pouting contentedly, eyes narrowed behind his strong, "intellectual's" glasses. Marie-Claude's plain little face, the colour of clay, with long green eyes in it, was lowered. She crumbled a piece of bread, for no obvious reason, and pushed her plate away.

"We had a lecture on Charlet at the Ecole du Louvre this afternoon," she said, to change the subject.

But Gérard was not letting his titbit go. He interrupted her. "Do you girls know what Nietzsche said—ironically? 'Women are always cats. Cats or birds, or cows when all is well!' Good, isn't it?"

Elisabeth put a hand to her forehead. "I'm not hungry any more; I've got a headache. I'm going to lie down for a bit."

"Oh dear—don't you want any pudding?" asked Mme Fonsèque, concerned.

"No."

"You'll come back soon, won't you?"

"Maybe."

Sobered, Gérard watched his eldest sister rise and go to the door, thin and erect in her maroon wool dress. She walked like a young man, with long strides.

She opened the door, went to her room, and sat down at her

pine table, which had no books or papers on it. She rested her head on her large, cold hands and closed her eyes.

How she hated such conversations! They appeared to be talking about Luce, but it was her they meant. When Mme Fonsèque stood up for the young couple, it was by way of reproaching herself, Elisabeth, for not marrying Tellier. When Gérard mocked the institution of marriage it was by way of congratulating herself, Elisabeth, on refusing Tellier's proposal. She was surrounded by veiled allusions, caught in a net of them like a fly in a spider's web. Still, she preferred her mother's unspoken disapproval to the pugnacious high spirits Gérard had taken to displaying recently. He was pleased with her for doing as he advised. He was pretending to think she was happy. His voice soothed her as if she were a docile mare who had just gone over a jump and was galloping away, relieved and panting hard. Well, she didn't want him interfering in her personal life any more! Nor anybody else either! Being the object of all this attention was infuriating. Luce had made her own decision; Luce had chosen for herself. Why hadn't they treated her in the same way as her sister?

She remembered Gérard sitting on the edge of the bed beside her, talking to her with careful kindness. "You see, the very fact that you're wavering proves you don't love Tellier. And since you don't love him you ought not to marry him. It wouldn't be fair to him, and it wouldn't be fair to yourself."

If he had been angry and shouted at her, no doubt she would have done as she pleased. But he seemed so reasonable, so kindly and earnest. It did not enter her head that he might be lying, or mistaken. It was true, in fact, that she did not love Joseph Tellier at the time. It was true that she felt bored in his company, and the idea of being his wife sometimes seemed a good one, but·sometimes did not. It had taken the rift between them, the inevitable coolness, and then Luce's sudden marriage, to make her regret her refusal. That was scarcely three months ago, and now she could not think of him without a tug at her heartstrings.

He was fifteen years older than she was, and limped slightly.

25

Gérard considered him ugly, coarse and uneducated. It was rumoured that he had been known to have a pretty little bit on the side in the Fonsèque's shop, which he managed. But such criticisms faded from her mind when she remembered his heavy, worn, weary face turned towards her in the yellow-lit bar, and his voice, hoarse with sadness, murmuring, "I understand, Elisabeth, I quite understand." Meanwhile, his fingers—masculine fingers with short nails and rough skin—were snapping potato crisps lying in a dish. At that moment she felt marvellously loved and desired. She knew that anything she said would affect him; he was her prey, panting before her, head lowered. She felt so sorry for him, yet all the same she went on speaking, implacable and serene.

"I've always thought of you as a friend. In fact, your proposal quite took me by surprise . . ."

Before they parted, she gave him her hand. He had kissed it, bending awkwardly to do so, and his jacket knocked over a glass on the table. The waiter had come running. It was she who had said, "It's all right—never mind."

How he must have suffered! How he must still be suffering! She thought of him in the dusty shop cluttered with cardboard cartons, or his own little room, which he had often described to her. A cold meal would be waiting for him on the kitchen table, with a note from the cleaning woman slipped under his glass. There would be the percolator, juddering on the stove, a wireless set indistinctly playing operetta choruses, and Tellier himself sitting down to eat, to smoke a cigarette—tired, at a loose end. And so lonely.

She pitied him with a kind of tender passion which filled her eyes with tears and constricted her throat pleasantly. She felt an urgent need arise in her to see him, comfort him, say yes to him. She could have spoken to him at Luce's wedding, but he had merely shaken hands politely and then left. No doubt he was afraid of seeing her again. No doubt, by now, he was trying to forget her? Well, it was all over. What might have been never would be, now. Would there be someone else for her? She wasn't like Luce, not one to marry the first comer. She would

26

keep her passion and her hunger to herself, and plan out her solitude. Where was Luce now? Staying in some big Venetian hotel with Paul. Sharing the same room, the same wash-basin, the same bed. A man's voice in her ear, a man's hands on her waist, a man's mouth on her mouth, the weight of a man on her body. Why her, thought Elisabeth, why her and not me? She's younger than I am, she's a silly creature, how can she make a man happy? While I, I . . .

She got up, and threw herself on her bed, arms crossed and face buried in the pillow. Her cheeks felt hot, the blood was pulsing in her clenched jaws. But she shed no tears, only sobbed dully, her throat tight and her eyes dry.

There was no earthly use in conjuring up the ridiculous image of Tellier's gnarled fingers breaking the potato crisps in their dish, yet she could not rid herself of it. It was very pleasant and very melancholy to remember his big hand aimlessly snapping crisps while she talked to him, destroying her own chances, making unhappiness for both of them. She could smell smoke and his skin when he was close to her: a male smell. Luce was living and sleeping in such an atmosphere. It wasn't fair! She wanted her share of pleasure too, she wanted it now. What did it matter if she had to sacrifice her own personality, as threatened by Gérard? It must be delightful to stupefy oneself with pleasure, be submissive and imitative, all in a kind of daze! To have a master.

Elisabeth, the proud, obstinate and determined Elisabeth wanted a master.

She sat on the edge of her bed; the wardrobe mirror showed her the reflection of a tall girl with her hair disarranged, skirt riding up above her knees, arms hanging, pale blotches marking her face as if she had just been wrestling with a tender but vigorous opponent.

She told herself to calm down. In three days' time, Tellier would visit them as usual to bring the monthly accounts from the shop. She would manage to get away from her office by six, and take a taxi home. She would say something kind to him.

Then perhaps he might realize she regretted her behaviour. He might ask if he could see her again?

Steps were coming down the corridor. She was on her feet in a flash, and when Mme Fonsèque opened the door she was sitting at her table, back straight, face expressionless, with an open book in front of her.

*   *   *

Elisabeth saw Joseph Tellier's hat and coat hanging in the hall. So he was still here. She was going to see him. Later this very evening, when she passed the hall mirror, which was surmounted by a stuffed stag's head with one eye missing, "something would have changed". It was a habit dating from her childhood for her to set herself this landmark. She went over to the door and took hold of the wooden knob. She was so weak that she felt sick. A sense of dull distress obliterated all thought from her mind. She opened the door.

She immediately felt the force of the shock she had both hoped for and feared. There he was, sitting in front of her mother, with his back to the doorway. He turned round. She saw his strong face, pale as indiarubber, with its bright little magpie eyes. His black hair was cut very short. One of his shoulders was lower than the other. A lighted cigarette clung to his lip.

"Good evening, Elisabeth."

She shook hands. She felt as if she were living in a dream, in a strange atmosphere where she was hardly in command of her own movements.

"Am I in the way?" she murmured.

He shook his head. So did her mother. Suddenly, she felt that some catastrophe was imminent. Something had happened; she didn't know what it was, she was going to find out, she didn't want to find out. Mme Fonsèque was already saying, in a neutral tone, "Do you know what Monsieur Tellier's just told me? He's got the offer of a very good post out in the country. He wants to hand over the management of the shop to someone else."

She thought she must have heard wrong. "What?"

"It's all right, I've found a replacement," said Tellier.

For a moment she was quite stunned. She was having difficulty in breathing, and was trembling from head to foot. It had taken just a few seconds to put everything back in the balance again. He was escaping her just when she hoped to win his love back, running away from her just when she realized she wanted to go to him. If he was planning to give up managing the shop and leave Paris, it must be so as to forget her. That was the way he had thought; that was how he preferred it.

Tellier was speaking, his voice hoarse but calm. "An excellent young man; he's a friend of my cousin Andoche."

"Oh, but you must stay!" Mme Fonsèque interrupted. "I've grown so used to working with you. I trusted you implicitly—I mean, the accounts here were only an excuse for a friendly visit! I'm sure this man you mention is a very good sort of person, but I don't know him, I'll have to keep an eye on what he does, and you must know how hard that'll be for me!"

What was the use of these sentimental arguments? No one was going to make Tellier change his mind; you only had to look at him to know that. His face was set in a tremendous effort of will, his body solid as a rock as he sat on the chair with his clenched fists on his knees.

Elisabeth leaned against the wall. Her head was beginning to swim slightly. There he was, near her. She only had to put out her hand to touch him. But this was the last time they would ever see each other. She had imagined a blissful reconciliation; now she had to think of something quite different: her future without him; dull days at the office; meals eaten at a table where Gérard would pontificate between mouthfuls ("Oh, do you know this aphorism of Nietzsche's?"); family evenings in the dimly lit drawing room; then the unbearable loneliness of her bedroom, her narrow bed, the wardrobe containing no clothes but her own, the wash-basin with no toilet things but her own, and there she would sleep at night all by herself in an old maid's narrow isolation.

Mme Fonsèque was still talking, plaintively. "Do you feel we've not been paying you an adequate salary?"

"No, no, nothing like that!"

"You see, in the present state of the business . . ."

Why wouldn't she go away and leave them alone together? Threats, prayers, supplication were called for, but there was Mme Fonsèque's lukewarm little voice still trotting out the same arguments!

"I know the prospects aren't anything much, but I did rather hope . . ."

He shrugged his shoulders and looked at his watch. It was all coming to an end. Even if she had found herself alone with him now, she could have thought of nothing more to say. Perhaps it was better for her mother to do the talking.

Her temples felt empty, and hurt her. The light was tiring her eyes. Only the pure, flat chill of the wall at her back made her aware of herself. All she wanted was for him to go away. Then she could relax, and think. What was he waiting for? If he stayed any longer she would cry out, run away, fall down! Oh, but these were the last few minutes he would ever spend with her, weren't they? She ought to want him to stay there in the drawing room as long as possible. No—she wished he would go, she wished he would go!

When he rose to say goodbye she moved slowly and stiffly away from the wall maintaining an expression of moderate interest and decent reserve on her face by a great effort of will.

"Well, do come and see us again before you leave, if only to introduce the new manager to me," Mme Fonsèque was saying. "Elisabeth, will you show Monsieur Tellier out?"

In the hall, he took down his hat and coat without looking at her. This was probably the last thing she would ever see him do. It was what she would remember in her empty nights. She suddenly recollected the mirror; she had promised herself to look in it when she came out of the room, when "something would have changed" . . .

The thought acted on her like an electric shock. She stepped towards him and whispered in a toneless voice, "Are you going because of me?"

Had she really spoken? His hand was on the doorknob. He turned. She saw his set face in the shadows, eyes narrowed and moist, mouth open.

"Yes," he said.

"Oh, you mustn't!"

"Why not?"

"I don't want you to."

He was so close now that she could smell his breath and the odour of his clothes. "Why would you want me to stay?"

"You'd be here."

"You never see me these days!"

"But I'd like it if I *was* seeing you again."

She had expected to feel terribly ashamed when she uttered those words, yet it was almost pleasant to say them. "I *will* see you again, won't I?" she whispered.

He tossed his hat and coat on a chair and passed a trembling hand over his forehead. The thought of the little shop assistant he had taken as his mistress after Elisabeth refused him flashed through his mind. Marcelle Audipiat: dark, skinny, sharp-tongued. He must break with her, sack her if necessary.

"Why are you telling me this now?" he sighed.

"Is it too late?"

"No, but . . ."

"Will you meet me from my office at six tomorrow? Oh, please go now!"

He had taken Elisabeth's hands and was looking at her with eyes full of surprise and delight. She was extraordinarily, deeply moved. Then he kissed her long, wiry fingers and the dry skin of her wrist. She whispered shakily, "Go away now— please!"

She was utterly exhausted. When the door closed behind him, she felt as if she had been knocked over the head.

III

Gérard tore up the sheet of paper, crumpled it into a ball, and threw it into the waste-paper-basket. His translation was going badly. He despised the work: meddling in bad novels at second hand. But it was an excuse not to take any job which would have removed him from home. Under cover of this pretext, he was preparing for the immense if vague literary work which was surely coming to fruition within him.

He leaned back in his chair. Although it was still daylight outside, he had closed the shutters and switched the light on. He felt better fortified against the world when he did not see the light of day. The objects surrounding him had taken on the friendly character of living things: the plaster skull, whose blank eye sockets he had once filled in with ink, the close-packed books of different sizes, his papers spread over the table. The room was preserved in silence as if in aspic. No noise could be heard in the apartment. Mme Fonsèque was out visiting, Elisabeth was at the office, Marie-Claude was at her lectures at the Ecole du Louvre. But he knew what time they would all be back.

He rose and went out into the chilly corridor.

He and his sisters had gathered in this corridor a few days after their father's death. Elisabeth, who was ten at the time, had told them you always found bloodstains in the room where a dead person had spent his last night. Although they had been forbidden to enter M. Fonsèque's room, she had sneaked in, accompanied by Gérard. The Venetian blinds were closed, and the air smelled musty, like the inside of an old cupboard. A picture was hanging crooked. Gérard thought he saw a trail of something dark staining the leather sofa. He ran out of the room, screaming. Later on, Marie-Claude and Luce shared this bedroom.

He opened the door. Luce's bed had been taken down to the

basement, and Marie-Claude's stood between the two bedside tables, which were piled with movie magazines and canvas-covered exercise books. Photographs of actors hung on the walls, framing the two reproductions of the *Raft of the Medusa* and the *Abduction of Proserpine*. Invitation cards were stuck in the groove around the mirror, with studied carelessness. There was a gramophone on the table (recently, Marie-Claude had decided to "polish up her languages" with the aid of Linguaphone courses), as well as an African statuette and an extensive collection of pencil sharpeners of every shape and colour. She was immensely proud of this collection. "Isn't it terrific?" she used to say, showing it off to her friends. There was also a small, stuffed toy dog, with a torn ear, placed on a chair; no one was allowed to touch this dog, or she would flare up, shouting, "You leave Mathurin-Jérôme alone!" A typical young girl's room—silly, pretentious and delightful. It irresistibly conjured up an idea of its owner, with her passionate crazes for "the handsomest man in the world", her sudden desire to learn Yugoslavian, or pottery, her pathetic little girlish secrets all carefully confided to her diary, her endearing fear of what the future held, along with a certainty that all the same, she was "someone".

The room next door was Elisabeth's. It had pale wallpaper and curtains hanging straight down. The floor was bare wood. Its monastic neatness stopped you in the doorway. Gérard leaned back against Elisabeth's wardrobe and closed his eyes for a moment.

He liked to visit his sisters' rooms while they were out. It was as if he were catching them unawares in their intimate being. The rooms where they slept, the air they had breathed unfailingly conjured them up to him. He would have done anything to increase his knowledge of them! When they were away from him, they ran countless well-defined dangers from which he would have protected them. He remembered how, as a child, he used to be afraid to watch them come downstairs or cross the road. He always imagined them carelessly taking a false step, twisting an ankle, falling down. It was still the same.

He was particularly worried about Elisabeth. He did not feel sure of her, and could not keep from checking up on his power over her. At dinner yesterday evening, when they were discussing Joseph Tellier's departure, he had expressed exaggerated satisfaction so as to get a clearer notion of the way his eldest sister reacted. "How can you be so horrid?" Marie-Claire had whispered, but Elisabeth herself showed no revealing signs of distress. She sat there, hard, silent, intelligent, taking no notice of the conversation. You would have thought the man meant nothing to her. Perhaps she really did not mind knowing he was unhappy, yet her faultless behaviour in itself disturbed Gérard. It was too good to be true. It must be hiding something. That nagging doubt he had felt yesterday was with him again. Indeed, he sought out subjects for alarm, as if tranquillity was not his proper element.

He went back to his room and flung himself down across the bed.

Abruptly, a memory came back to him: that summer evening when Vigneral, claiming that he was going to widen his friend's horizons and provide him with some new impressions, took him to a brothel in the Boulevard de la Chapelle. Girls clad in filmy fabrics were dancing together, their heavy hips swaying, and the air was full of the scent of warm female flesh and face-powder. Vigneral watched the lamentable performance with an expression of cynical susceptibility on his face, a mixture of pleasure and distaste. Gérard remembered the dimly-lit little room, too, and the strange face bent over his. The girl's large eyes were tired, her skin seemed to be stiff with cosmetics, her heavy, opened mouth with its cracking lipstick smelled strongly of smoke and food. She chanted words in a monotonous voice, like a litany: "Don't you worry, darling, it'll be all right . . . I bet you've been on the spree, with a pretty face like that! Want a cigarette? No? You're off, then?"

He rapidly banished this image, and the memory of her distasteful chant, which haunted him. Love wasn't like that; love was above such monkey tricks! Woman was not that writhing monster, submissively offered up. Love-making was not the sinuous, smooth, dreary movement of one body against another from which one's spirit was miles away. One does not make love in the same way as one eats and drinks and sleeps, but in a communion which transfigures our baser needs. Surely a mysterious harmony between the animal appetites and the highest of spiritual aspirations can come into existence between two superior beings! A miraculous attraction sublimates instinct. Man and Woman escape the shackles of the flesh, without sacrificing any of their wealth of feeling. Luce had failed to understand this basic truth, but she would be sorry later. (She might even be sorry now!) "Paul adores me! I adore Paul! I'm out of my mind with happiness!" Words, just words! Now, if only Lequesne could have courted and married his sister, how happily he would have promoted their union! But Lequesne had no strength of character, despite his deistic theories. Only a beaten man trusts to chance! Mustn't forget to tell him that. Gérard took out a notebook and wrote the phrase down.

Four walls, a window with the shutters slightly ajar, and you can be happy in isolation, thought Gérard. Solitude allows you to believe in your genius. It's the presence of other people that cuts you down to their own puny size. But in the cessation of all noise and movement, what sublime impulses may raise us to our rightful level! That must be supreme happiness, that reinvigorated certitude, that blissful suspension of consciousness. No doubts, no regrets, no hopes. Lequesne would have said it was God on your side, but there was nothing divine about such felicity. It had a terrestrial reason. It was the worker's exhausted satisfaction.

Gérard's heart was beating fast, and he was bathed in sweat, although he had been lying perfectly still.

Lequesne's mysticism was rather short-sighted. God was not mixed up in everyday life! At most, God's influence might be perceived at the milestones of one's life, but in between times, Man was free to go whatever way he liked.

Gérard lit a cigarette. The smoke drifted towards the half-open window. In a similar manner, he thought, all our actions

35

flow towards the same end, but it's up to us to divert the course of them for a moment or so. One breath, and a thousand movements disturb the vaporous river before it flows away into the greedy dark.

He went over to the window, pushed back the shutters, and breathed in that cold, vast darkness.

The Place des Vosges, with its garden a blur of vegetation, its little houses neatly arranged in a rectangle, its softly-lit window panes, might have been straight from another era.

He would not allow himself to evoke thoughts of Théophile Gautier, Victor Hugo or Marion Delorme; he hated literary commonplaces. To act, to create, to venture on something new—that was the thing! He would start writing his philosophical essay on Evil tomorrow. "Chapter One: The ideas of Good and Evil as related to the pleasant and the unpleasant." That was a good phrase! The cold air chilled his forehead.

He was about to withdraw from the window when two familiar figures came out of the square, walking slowly towards the arcades. He shot abruptly backwards.

Elisabeth and Tellier, arm in arm like any couple of vulgar lovers! So she was seeing him again! She still loved him! The revelation drained Gérard of all his strength. He heard ringing in his ears, and his heart beat fast, labouring as if he had been climbing a slope.

He stood leaning against the table for a long time, his head held high, his eyes narrowed in an expression of grim watchfulness.

*   *   *

Mme Fonsèque entered her bedroom, switched on the light, and stopped in surprise. Gérard stood there facing her, hands in his pockets, face pale and haggard, a thin lock of hair falling over his forehead. He had left the dining room when dessert was served, saying he had some urgent work to finish.

"Goodness, what are you doing here?" she asked.

"Shut the door. I must talk to you."

Hastily, she obeyed him, fearing some bad news. He had lit a cigarette. She did not like to see him smoke, but she stopped herself saying so.

"Did you know Elisabeth's been seeing Tellier again?" he asked, in level tones.

She heaved a sigh of relief. So that was all! "Oh, yes, she's just this moment told me! And apparently he's willing to stay on as manager, too!"

"I might have known it!" Gérard gave a snort of laughter. "So she chose to announce the news when I was out of the room! Cowardly, but clever. What did you tell her?"

"I told her I was very pleased! It would have meant a lot of bother for me, Joseph Tellier leaving."

"She must have been very persuasive, to get him to change his mind."

"Yes, I expect she was."

His mouth twisted in disgust. "How ignoble!"

"Why?"

"Well, what's he going to suppose now?"

"He'll suppose we think a great deal of him."

"He'll suppose *she* thinks a great deal of him!"

"What if she does?"

He thumped the table with his fist. "How do you mean; what if she does? Buoyed up by that certainty, he'll pester and pursue her—and propose to her again. And fool that I know she is, she might even accept him this time!"

Mme Fonsèque had sat down in her armchair. "Oh, don't shout!" she whispered. "She might hear you!"

"What's she doing?"

"She's in her room. I expect she's asleep."

"Asleep and dreaming!" he groaned. "With your maternal blessing on her head! What a crying shame it is!"

"I don't see any harm in it myself!"

"You don't see any harm in it! You never do! You didn't see any harm in it with Luce either! You think your mission in life is to throw your three daughters into anyone's arms and

37

anyone's bed just as soon as you possibly can!"

"Gérard, really!"

He lowered his voice to a whisper. "You simply cast them adrift, and you don't mind where they end up!"

He did feel he was going rather far, but a cruel frenzy egged him on to wound her.

"You're laying up unhappiness for your children, with a good shopkeeper's satisfied smile!"

"Be quiet, Gérard! You don't know what you're saying!" Much upset, and near tears, Mme Fonsèque shook her big, fleshy head and clasped her hands.

He felt sorry for what he had said at once. She did not deserve to be attacked like that, and it had been clumsy of him, too. Far better to win her over gently, lull her with sweet reason. But how could he master the anger that consumed him at the mere thought of the marriage? How could he justify what he saw as the deplorable nature of the facts?

He sat down on a chair beside her. The room around them seemed to be listening, an old-fashioned bedroom with its flowered wallpaper and mahogany furniture. He breathed in the scent of eau de cologne and withered apples, familiar to him from childhood. The bed was made up, with a voluminous pink nightdress spread out on the pillow. He remembered Mme Fonsèque, fifteen years ago, saying, "We'll have to live on a smaller scale now," and he had pictured her sitting on a little pair of scales. He smiled at that long-ago memory, and laid a hand on his mother's arm.

"Now, Mother, listen to me."

She jumped. How scared of him she was! It was both pleasant and alarming to have such power over her.

He went on, kindly. "I've thought this over carefully. We have no right to let Elisabeth marry that man."

"She's free to choose."

"Yes, of course. But just now her choice wouldn't really be a free one. It's Luce's marriage that's caused the trouble. Elisabeth is upset because Luce got married first. She's afraid of being left on the shelf, so she's ready to throw herself at the

38

first comer. That's not love, it's pride. Competitive pride! She's playing at emulating Luce . . . I mean, if she really loved Tellier, she wouldn't have refused him three months ago!"

"You advised her to refuse him."

"Well, she took my advice, so she must have thought it was good!"

Mme Fonsèque mopped her face with her handkerchief. Whenever her son began arguing with her, she felt as if she had lost the argument already, as if his words were a web that he cast around her, gradually immobilising her. However, she put up an honourable resistance.

"She'll hate us if we show we're against it . . ."

"Won't she hate us even more when the first raptures have worn off, and she finds herself tied to a man she married out of spite?"

He was so obviously wrong, and yet she did not know just why. She could find no answer. "But all the same," she whispered, "all the same . . ."

He had risen to his feet. "You'll have to speak to her!"

She made one more brave if futile effort to resist.

"I wouldn't dream of it! Poor child, she's unhappy! I don't want to upset her!"

But Gérard's voice was going implacably on. "She'd do far better to wait for another husband . . . she doesn't want to ruin her whole life for a hasty impulse . . . they'd soon feel all the effects of it . . ." Then came that metaphor he liked so much, about helping a blind man to cross the road. Gérard had an answer for everything. She was vanquished, overcome, unable to see straight any more. Suddenly she found herself hoping he was right, because she knew she was going to do as he said. In any case, why wouldn't he be right? He loved his sisters. He wanted them to be happy.

Her face was very close to his, and she saw how bloodless it was, tensed in a formidable effort of will. Gérard's masterful eyes were fixed on hers. But now he had defeated her she was not afraid of him. She felt he was exhausted and on edge, and was vaguely sorry for him.

"You could speak to her after dinner tomorrow, for instance," he said.

"She won't listen to me."

"She listened to *me*, the first time!"

The good lady felt a faint flicker of hope. "Then why don't you speak to her yourself?"

"Because she doesn't trust me! She thinks I have a grudge against Tellier. But you've always been on her side — what you say will carry more weight with her."

She tried to think of a reply, failed, and sat there for a moment, rubbing her knees with both hands. Gérard, feeling breathless, his shirt sticking to his collarbones, looked at her, her head bent in pensive obedience. There was a narrow parting in her greying hair. The frown had left her forehead. She was not upset any more, she had stopped resisting. He had won.

"So I can count on you, can I?"

"What am I to say to her?" she asked.

IV

Sitting at his table, Gérard strained his ears, listening to the humming silence of the apartment building. However, he could not make out the distant voices of Elisabeth and his mother. They had been in the little sitting room for an hour now, talking. He had brought his mother up to scratch, poor soul. She would run verbatim through the charges he had drummed into her the previous evening. But Elisabeth was well able to defend herself; he could not be sure of anything. All this agitation and anxiety tired him. He folded the skirts of his old, plum-coloured dressing-gown round his legs, and sipped tea from the cup before him. The papers spread out on the table attracted his attention. He leafed through the beginning of his translation, but looked away from it almost at once.

The lamp, with its green shade, diffused an underwater light. The whole room was sharing his nocturnal vigil. Eleven o'clock. He imagined his sister and his mother locked in combat, the outcome still uncertain. It gave him palpitations just to imagine their two faces, one fleshy, frank and imploring, the other hard as stone. He put his fingers to his sweating cheeks. He was panting with the effort the other two were making, worn out by their exhaustion, concentrating on a struggle at which he was not present.

Suddenly, a door squealed. Elisabeth's footsteps came down the corridor. He thought she was going to her bedroom, but she had already passed it. Gérard rose, his legs stiff, intending to get hastily into bed, lie down and pretend to be asleep. He was too late. The door swung back against the wall, and there stood Elisabeth.

She held her head high, like a snake about to strike. Her arms were dangling at the sides of her thin body. It was her eyes, a cold and candid grey, that delivered the first blow.

He had stepped back against the wall.

"This is between you and me," she said flatly.

He bowed his head, accepting the challenge.

"I've just been having a discussion with Mother."

"You have?" But next moment he decided that lying was no use. "Yes, I know," he added.

"You asked her to speak to me—you needn't bother to deny it! Listening to her, I could practically hear your voice. I recognized your own style of spitefulness!"

"I'm not denying anything."

"You weren't brave enough to speak to me yourself."

"Well, were you brave enough to tell me, to my face, you were seeing Tellier again? You started this little game when I was out of the room, so it was only fair to finish it the same way."

She shrugged her rather broad shoulders and shook her head. "Never mind your verbal fencing—keep it for your arguments with Lequesne. All I have to say to you can be put into a few words. I am not having you interfering in my life. I think I'm old enough to choose my own course of conduct. Tellier proposed to me again at six this evening, and I decided to accept him. I shall marry Joseph Tellier, I shall marry him in spite of you, and your insinuations may well come between you and me, but not between me and him!"

"Although if I remember correctly, they did come between the two of you a couple of months ago, didn't they?"

"Because I didn't love him then."

"And now?"

"Now I do."

"You mean it happened just like that, all of a sudden?"

"Yes."

"You know, this urge to get married is something that's come over you since Luce's wedding. You didn't want to be left on the shelf! You wanted a man!"

"There's no need to try making my feelings sound dirty when you're incapable of any such feelings yourself!"

"Thank God for that!"

Elisabeth took hold of the back of a chair, clutching the

42

polished wood as if it were a human arm. "Now you listen to me, Gérard," she said quietly. "I came here hoping to make things up with you. I wanted to tell you how silly your dislike of Tellier is—and even if you don't like him, you have no right to destroy my happiness for your own selfish reasons. For the last time, I'm asking you to stop being so supercilious and disapproving, and then I'll forget this whole incident."

He simply whistled a few shrill notes.

"You won't then?" she asked.

"No."

"Very well, I've tried my best, and now I'm going."

She took a step towards the door.

"Now you're listening to me!" he said. He was standing in the doorway, so that she could not get out.

"Are you going to stop me leaving?"

"Before I've had my say, you mean? Yes, I am."

He looked at her; she gave the impression of being rather taller than usual. Her eyes shone in the deep of their sockets, and the light surrounded her loosened hair with an aureole. Uneven breathing raised her breasts under her straight dress. He had never before been aware of such direct dislike.

"Just now you hate me, Elisabeth," he said. "But honestly, I'm acting in your own interests! Surely you know I'm not opposed to your getting married in principle, as you seem to think? I just don't want you to marry Tellier."

"I couldn't care less!"

"And the reason I don't want you to marry him is that he's not good enough for you."

"That's for me to judge, thank you."

"The trouble is, you *can't* judge at the moment, because you claim to be in love with him, so it's for me to open your eyes, and then you'll have to admit I'm right."

"Gérard, please let me by."

"Afraid I'll shatter your illusions?"

"I'm afraid you'll say something you may regret later."

"That's very thoughtful of you, but it doesn't cut any ice with me! Now listen, Elisabeth. When I think of your marriage,

43

what do I see? On the one hand a beautiful girl—intelligent, cultivated, made for all kinds of higher satisfactions, and on the other . . ."

"Stop it, Gérard!"

She had uttered these words in strangled tones. Her face, in the lamplight, looked pale, frightened and frightening. So he'd struck home! Gérard went remorselessly on, quivering with pleasure, emphasizing his words, carefully calculating his tone of voice to hurt, "And on the other hand, a man like Joseph Tellier. Our manager. An uneducated shopkeeper, without any money, without any talents . . ."

He guessed he was wounding her with every word he spoke. She had moved closer to him. He had a clear view of her pale forehead, a vertical vein standing out on it. Her eyes were sparkling with anger, and her thin, bloodless lips were pressed together, their corners trembling nervously.

"You're disgusting," she said.

"Look, you're so besotted you just haven't thought of anything but the immediate future. But think of the *distant* future awaiting you! A whole lifetime with Tellier. Meals with Tellier, evenings with Tellier. Tellier caressing you. Tellier first thing in the morning, with his hair rumpled, and bad breath. Tellier in his underpants!"

"Be quiet, Gérard!"

"Tellier telling you his dirty little shopkeeper's tricks at mealtimes. Tellier kissing you between mouthfuls, with his lips all greasy and crumbs on his trousers!"

She made for the door. He seized her wrists, shouting, "And Tellier taking off his cripple's built-up shoe before he goes to bed: And Tellier *in* bed . . ."

She had broken free, and abruptly she slapped his face.

He did not move. He felt nauseated, dizzy, faint; he saw her face, almost unrecognizable, illuminated and made beautiful by hatred.

He felt as if her silent lips were actually shining. He thought his knees were going to give way under him, but he still had strength enough to murmur, "Well, at least you've had a piece of my mind, my girl!"

V

The maid preceded Vigneral down the corridor. "Monsieur Gérard won't be long. If you wouldn't mind waiting a moment, I'll let Mademoiselle Marie-Claude know you're here . . ."

She opened a door and stood aside for the tall young man, square-shouldered, slim-hipped, his beaky face crowned with untidy fair hair. His wet raincoat was open, revealing a casual suit gone rather baggy at the knees. His tie was crooked, and hung out of his waistcoat.

Vigneral went into Gérard's room and closed the door behind him. He did not care for the dark, overheated room, redolent of its reclusive occupant and of paper. There were too many books lining the walls, too many papers on the table. He put his coat down on the bed and went over to the bookshelves: Spinoza's *Ethics, Beyond Good and Evil* . . . he could never quite get used to the idea that he was friends with such a skinny, sallow, bespectacled fellow, who had read everything, seen nothing, and was proud of both his knowledge and his ignorance. Everything about him annoyed Vigneral. He disliked Gérard's way of wearing clothes too warm for the time of year, his habit of wiping his hand on his trouser leg before offering it to anyone, the revoltingly sweet cigarettes he smoked. Then there were the affectations he assumed when talking. (The way he liked to throw his head back, nostrils pinched and eyes narrowed! Marie-Claude told him, "You look like a reed, thinking.") There was his patronizing use of quotations, too: "You'd know, if you had read Nietzsche, that . . ." "According to Bergson's excellent definition of mysticism . . ." In fact, the mere sight of his friend made Vigneral want to talk in a loud voice, tell spicy stories, make unnecessary gestures with his arms and legs. But perhaps this was just why he liked to come and see Gérard.

They had got to know each other in their first year at

secondary school, during gym. Gérard, a new boy, was gazing in alarm at the gymnasium walls, bristling with healthful instruments of torture, and at the other shirtsleeved pupils, running on the spot and spitting on their hands before tackling the parallel bars or the trapeze. A whistle blew. "Fonsèque!" Gérard jumped for the rings, failed to reach them, and fell on the mat. Loud laughter greeted his fall. "Fonsèque's dumb, fell on his bum!" whispered the other boys. "Fonsèque, you display all the grace of an elephant walking the tightrope!" said the gym master, wittily. "Try again. Come on, then, jump to those rings! Bend your back! Tuck your bottom in!" Hanging by his hands and feet, mouth open, Gérard could see the other boys laughing and slapping their thighs. The master tapped his tense buttocks with a ruler. "Come along, now, come along!" Finally, the ultimate insult: "Here, Vigneral, come and show him how to exercise on the rings properly! Keep at it with him until he's fit to join in with the rest."

Their friendship dated from that day. Later, they used to exchange confidences and plans. Vigneral remembered the knowing conversations they had in class. At this period Fonsèque would air a supercilious if sketchy knowledge of sexual matters. He told wildly complicated stories about women, in an undertone, stories of which he was invariably the hero, featuring mysterious strangers—women friends of his mother's—who were just passing through Paris, had lured him to their rooms the previous evening, plied him with drink and taken lascivious advantage of him, with the result that he had not had time to do his geography homework. Or he talked about pale-faced girls, ladies' companions glimpsed behind the windows of town houses, to whom he wrote verses—in secret, but he was thinking of publishing these verses in volume form, since some of them were really very good. ("Rather a special sort of inspiration, if you see what I mean!") Vigneral remembered how his friend's eyes would shine feverishly in his sallow, pimply face with its dry lips; he himself used to turn his head aside to avoid Gérard's breath. Then Fonsèque took a different tack. Once they were in their last year at school, he claimed his utter lack of interest in "such pitiful glandular matters". ("I realize one must satisfy one's hunger now and then, but hunger must not be allowed to degenerate into greed.") It was after their final examinations that Vigneral took him to the brothel. Fonsèque had come out pale, sweating, and shrinking with disgust. Out in the street, they discussed diseases.

Vigneral lit a cigarette and went over to the window, which was blurred with rain. How could anyone enjoy a job like this? Chasing from office to office in such weather—and what for, for God's sake? He had sold only six boxes of carbon paper. He'd have just enough to pay for a taxi home when he'd been to see his girl this evening. Unless he stayed in bed with her until the underground trains started running in the morning, but he did not fancy the prospect of spending a whole night with Tina. She was a tall, dark girl, vivacious but breathtakingly stupid, and she bored him. Though born and bred in Paris, she affected a quacking American accent by virtue of being a barmaid in the Toc-Toc Cocktail Bar, frequently employing such phrases as, "Okay, darling?" and, "Honey, don't use that towel on the left for your face!" She was a tart, really.

He looked at his watch: six o'clock. He had decided to call on Fonsèque after his day's work selling stationery, but he had nothing much to say to him. When, come to think of it, did he last have anything much to say to him? If he's not back in fifteen minutes I'm going, he thought.

No sooner had he come to this decision than he heard quick footsteps in the corridor. The door opened and Marie-Claude came in, smiling, rather awkward, simply dressed in a long-sleeved grey jumper and a blue woollen skirt. He thought she was wearing more make-up than usual.

"You've turned up just in time!" said Vigneral. "I was dying of boredom in this literary incubator of Gérard's!"

"Oh, he's gone to see his publisher—he won't be long. Do sit down!"

He remained standing, looking her over with stolid calm.

47

There was nothing particularly attractive about her wan face, framed in lank hair, but her eyes soon caught your attention. They were very large, and their pupils were a pure leaf-green. He pointed a finger suddenly. "What on earth are those?"

He meant the four or five enamel brooches pinned to Marie-Claude's jumper.

"My badges! They're souvenirs from abroad and winter sports and so on."

"But you've never been abroad, have you? Or to winter sports?"

"Well, no."

"Then why wear them? It's silly."

She blushed, and thought crossly, for a moment, how stupid he was! But he was already shaking his head and passing a hand over his forehead. "Sorry—never mind! I'm glad to see you, badges and all! Thanks for coming to talk to me, specially if I've disturbed you. Were you working?"

"Just copying out my notes from the Ecole du Louvre."

"Aha, the Ecole du Louvre! A fine waiting room, isn't it? Good girls hang about there getting ready for Life, killing time!"

She decided to take offence. "You're quite wrong! I don't go to the lectures at the Louvre to kill time, I go because I'm interested in art history and I . . ."

His smile was broad and serene. "Come on, that's just an excuse!"

She thought he might be right, in which case it had been rather ridiculous of her to protest. Still—"You can't know!" she said.

"Oh yes, I can, my little Marie-Claude, oh yes, I can!"

She had always rather liked Vigneral's way of calling her "my little Marie-Claude". His outgoing self-assurance made her feel positively anxious to be wrong, and in need of care and protection. She thought, suddenly, that she would like to give him a box of cigarettes or a tie, and hear him scold her gently for giving such a present. She then immediately decided that she must be quite mad, and a wave of heat rose to her face.

48

"You'll agree with me on your wedding day," Vigneral went on. "You'll realize that your present pursuits were just something to keep you waiting patiently. Like the magazines in the dentist's surgery—the documentary before the big film. Oh, by the way, about Elisabeth's marriage . . ."

Gratefully, she seized upon his change of subject. "My goodness, what a fuss. Life in this place has become unbearable! Elisabeth and Tellier won't hear of a church wedding, and it's making Mother quite ill. She feels it's a disgrace, and she keeps on about the memory of Father and Uncle Charles!"

"And how about Gérard?"

"Gérard's not a bit interested. He had a quarrel with Elisabeth—I don't know what about—and they haven't been speaking since! They don't even say good morning to each other. When Mother asks Tellier to dinner, Gérard makes sure he's going out to spend the evening with Lequesne. It's like that the whole time! And here am I on my own, with everyone else in such a state of nerves—honestly, I just don't know how to behave!"

She spoke with a quaint air of disenchantment which suited her very well. Unsure what to do with her hands, which were rather red, their wrists still bony like a little girl's, she let them dangle, palms outward, in the folds of her skirt, and when she saw him looking at them put them slowly behind her back.

Vigneral was rather enjoying the curious sensation this visit gave him. Last night he had been lying in bed with a naked, vulgar, demanding woman, kissing her mouth till they were both breathless, breathing in her scent, feeling her all over. And now, with only a day's work in between the two episodes, here he was talking to this child: a well-brought-up child, rather silly and slightly in love with him. He expected Marie-Claude thought about him when she went to bed. She probably started when someone mentioned him in her hearing. She probably kept some old photograph or other of himself and Gérard at school in a folder. She might even keep a diary! Suddenly, he interrupted her.

49

"You've certainly got a lot to write about in your diary!"

She jumped. "How did you know I keep one?"

Delighted, he kept his head bent so that she wouldn't see him smile. "Oh Gérard told me."

"I've never shown it to him."

"No, but he found it lying about your room one day."

"He didn't read it, did he?"

"Yes, he did."

She was confused and panic-stricken. "Oh, how beastly of him!" she breathed.

"Are you cross? Have you got so many shocking things to record in it?"

(Obviously there were pages and pages of high-flown sentiments about himself! What wouldn't he give to read that diary!)

"It's nothing to do with you!"

Then he realized that she had tears in her eyes, and her chin was trembling. It would not take much more to make her burst into tears, slam the door and escape to her room, to fling herself on the bed and bury her face in the bolster. He made haste to reassure her.

"It's all right, I'm only joking! Just pulling your leg! Gérard never told me about your diary!"

"Then who did?"

"Nobody."

"You just guessed?"

"Yes."

It had been a close shave. She was looking at him through wet lashes, her lips parted. It suddenly struck him that she was charming.

"You're horrible!" she said.

He had risen to his feet; he burst out laughing. She began to laugh too, a stifled, gasping laughter that shook her shoulders.

At this moment the door behind them opened and Gérard came into the room. Marie-Claude uttered a cry. "Oh, how you scared me! I didn't hear you coming."

He smiled, wanly.

"So I see," he remarked.

VI

There were too many sandwiches on the table, which was surrounded by a noisy group of guests. (The night before, Mme Fonsèque and the maid had sat in the kitchen hard at work cutting bread, buttering it, filling the sandwiches with slices of ham and cheese and putting them away in tins for the night, while Marie-Claude kept swooping down on the little crusts that piled up on the greaseproof paper.) On the other hand, there was not enough to drink. The champagne was already running out. The maid, in a panic, had suggested orangeade, which was diluted behind the scenes. The wood of the table's extension leaves had warped, so that there were humps underneath the cloth. Apart from these minor drawbacks, however, the wedding reception was a definite success. Even Gérard was being wonderfully polite, although it had been feared he might make a scene.

Mme Fonsèque, standing back in the bay of a window, was watching the progress of the reception with the expression of an eagle-eyed hostess ready to notice ash falling on the carpet, a wet glass put down on a whatnot, somebody nudging a broken cup under the divan with his foot, while she still wore a constant smile and had her hand held out to welcome guests or say goodbye.

She had insisted on having a very simple reception at home after the civil ceremony, and it was no more than right that she should get her way, since she had given in on the question of the church wedding. She was only afraid that her daughter would be upset by the contrast between this small gathering and the grand party the Aucocs had given for Luce. Elisabeth was so proud and remote! And hadn't she said, a few days earlier, that the over-expensive present sent by the Aucoc family was a veiled insult? Mme Fonsèque looked past the guests in search of her. She was talking to Luce and Paul. Good. And where

51

was Tellier? With M. Aucoc senior: excellent. Marie-Claude? Talking to Vigneral; well, never mind that. Where was Gérard?

She could not find him, wherever she looked, failing to spot his weary face, shining with moisture, hidden in the shadows by the doorway. The noise and the heat numbed him. He was resigned to it all now. He simply wanted to get back to his room, shut himself in, settle under his lamp with its green shade like some nocturnal bird, to be with his books and papers, not moving, not thinking of anything, just waiting for his feeling of sick depression to go away.

· Really, he had suffered more than he could bear during this single day! It was a cruel form of torture. There had been the waiting room in the city hall, with its red seats, gilded plasterwork, and two or three impatient families in their Sunday best, tense, muttering and dark-clad around the sugary white figure of the bride. Then couples were called in. The usher on duty would announce some grotesque name or other, and a whole collection of ladies-and-gentlemen would rise to file off in the direction of the door at the back. A formal "Who's next?" reminiscent of the dentist's surgery. Then, another and unremarkable room with a green table, the fat, bald mayor, the clerk opposite him, his bad colour suggesting a poor digestion. Elisabeth and Tellier sat facing the man, with his tricolor sash, their relatives behind them as if watching them receive an examination certificate. The chairs were still warm from the previous wedding party. What a sad sort of comedy it was: all this creaking regimentation surrounding the realities of flesh and blood! Signatures, paper-work, chatter, all leading up to those breathless nocturnal sports to come!

After the ceremony, Gérard had managed to bring himself to congratulate his sister and brother-in-law, after avoiding speaking to them at all for weeks. How deplorably pleased they had been! They were only too ready to forgive him any insults, wiping the slate clean with pathetic dexterity. They would forget it! Let's be friends, come what may—anything for a quiet life! His mother had been delighted by their reconciliation too. As if it had meant anything! As if he would ever be really reconciled to them, before he finally won!

He saw Mme Fonsèque looking his way. She had spotted him at last. Making a great effort, he moved away from the wall and went over to a group of guests. M. Aucoc senior and young Hurault were talking politics. M. Aucoc, crimson in the face and half stifled by his corset, was holding forth in an unctuous voice, as if addressing a public meeting.

"Like it or not, the Radicals are the ballast in the ship of state! Young people may attack them before they take all their difficulties into account—later, they'll enlist under their banner!"

"Never! What we want is maximum liberty with minimum authority, minimum self-indulgence with maximum security!" announced Hurault, with his mouth full.

"Our positions are not irreconcilable," said M. Aucoc.

Tiny little Mme Aucoc, got up like a circus pony and with her white hair arranged in ringlets, was telling an old lady with a face like a gargoyle, "Oh, I know, my dear! Why, I was getting out of the car yesterday when a young man, rather poorly dressed, like a student, came over and handed me a little leaflet—it was a song, called 'The Song of the Slums'. Well, I gave him five francs and took the song—I was going to play it on the piano when I got home, but this is how it went!

Let the bourgeois tremble
At his mansion gate!
The working people's anger
Will reach him soon or late!
Oho, oho, oho!
The workers will lay him low.

"Well, I mean to say, fancy the Government allowing a thing like that to be sold in the public streets!"

Luce and Paul came over. Luce was looking beautiful, dressed with slightly showy elegance, and her red hair drew all eyes as she passed. She moved, Gérard thought, with the softness of some lush plant, an abundant, gentle, feminine tranquility which was almost animal-like and made him want to slap her. Her husband, pink and plump as a piglet, followed snuffling along in her wake, snapping up her slightest word as if it were nourishment.

"Paul darling, could you fetch us some sandwiches?"

What a gulf was fixed between Luce and Gérard! They were strangers—worse than strangers, for between strangers, acquaintanceship and friendship remain possible. But there was no chance of any reconciliation between them now. And Elisabeth would turn out just the same. Mme Aucoc. Mme Tellier.

Paul was on his way back to them with a napkin full of sandwiches.

"Darling, doesn't the green of this salad remind you of anything?" he asked.

"No."

"Why, the donor's cloak, remember? In that little picture we liked so much in Venice!"

"Oh yes! Darling, you're amazing! Now, who was it by?"

Gérard turned on his heel, but only to come face to face with Tellier and Elisabeth as they moved away from the table. Tellier was dressed in black, his detachable collar in impeccable condition, but his face haggard with heat, fatigue and emotion. He was munching a *petit four*.

"You do look hot, Joseph dear!" said Elisabeth.

Gérard noticed the intimacy of her tone, her soft voice, her smile. Was she blind? Was everybody blind, except for him?

"Elisabeth, let me introduce my cousin Andoche . . ."

There was a squeal at the far end of the room: Marie-Claude had just dropped a sandwich, and was in fits of laughter, while Vigneral, standing beside her, patted her on the back to calm her down. Her exclamation and her laughter jarred on Gérard.

"Hullo, Fonsèque."

He turned. There was Lequesne, carefully shaved and with his tie neatly arranged, but lack-lustre of eye.

"You?" said Gérard. "I didn't think you'd come!"

"Why not?"

"Oh, I don't know—just an idea I had." Abruptly, he took Lequesne's arm. "Let's have a drink."

In passing, he jerked his chin towards Luce. "She came back from Italy a fortnight ago."

"Oh yes?"

"Seems to be happy."

"She looks happy."

"And in a state of total idiocy!"

"I suppose happy people do seem a bit idiotic to those who envy them."

"Do you want to speak to her?"

"Oh, don't bother . . . she's talking, she's busy . . ."

Once again Gérard guessed Lequesne was nurturing that melancholy resignation which was his undoing. "You know, Lequesne, I feel you just don't know how to work for your own happiness!" he said. "You don't make any effort. You just wait for it to fall into your lap."

They had reached the table.

"What makes you say that?" asked Lequesne.

"Oh, nothing in particular . . ."

"No?" Lequesne had picked up a sandwich from the pile, and was about to take a bite of it, but instead he held it out to Gérard. "Look here, Fonsèque. You may think this sandwich looks delicious. But if you'd cut the bread, and buttered it, and filled the sandwich yourself, perhaps you wouldn't want to eat it? Same thing with happiness! When you've worked for it yourself you're not so keen to enjoy it. Do you see what I mean?"

"Monsieur Lequesne?" said a musical voice.

He jumped. Luce was coming over to them.

"I'm so sorry—I didn't notice you," he muttered, feeling as if he were dropping a large brick.

"What was that you were saying about the sandwiches?"

"Me? Oh, nothing!"

He was red-faced and awkward before this beautiful girl, so full of confidence and grace.

"He was telling me he likes eating sandwiches better than

making them," said Gérard.

"Well, so does everyone!" exclaimed Luce.

"Apparently not," said Lequesne.

Luce looked at them, uncomprehendingly.

"Take no notice!" Gérard laughed. "We were talking metaphysics!" And he went off, shoulders hunched, hands in his pockets.

Mme Fonsèque detained him as he passed her. "How are you feeling, dear?"

"Oh, simply marvellous!"

He slipped out into the dark hall, which was full of coats. He needed to be alone to recover his spirits. The stupidity, the ugliness, the odour of these people oppressed him like something in a nightmare. Any one of them, taken individually, might be bearable, but when they were all together in a crowd you saw the bestiality of their faces, you heard the idiocy of their conversation. They showed each other up, reacting to each other, tossed about together, as it might be in a photographer's developing bath. "Darling, doesn't the green of this salad remind you of anything? . . . You do look hot, Joseph dear! . . . Maximum liberty with minimum authority . . ." Frowning, Gérard sank into a chair and leaned his head back against the cold wall.

He heard the sound of the lavatory flushing, and Tellier came out, checking his flies with a groping finger. Their eyes met. Gérard was never to forget that confused expression on Tellier's face, his clumsy, awkward attitude, his dangling arm. "Oh, did you want to go in?" asked Tellier, stupidly.

"Dear me, no."

There was a silence. Tellier smiled, embarrassed, and ill at ease to have been seen coming out of the lavatory. "Rather chilly out here—I'll be getting back in . . ."

Gérard followed him into the drawing room and watched, with a swelling heart, as he went over to Elisabeth and said something in her ear. Then they turned and began walking slowly to the door.

PART TWO

I

Gérard looked at his notebook. "Lequesne: Court C, Staircase 30, sixth on the left."

Dark doorways numbered 1 to 25 opened on little concrete-floored courtyards marked A, B, C, D. Each courtyard contained a sandbox for the children. There were little windows in the brick walls, like Judas eyes.

One of these windows belonged to Lequesne's apartment; Gérard could not remember which. He had only been to see his friend here a couple of times, and he had not said he was coming today. He had just felt a sudden urgent need to see him and talk to him. He could not stand the loneliness at home these days. It was in the evenings that he missed Luce and Elisabeth most. Empty chairs, an empty bedroom, an evening spent with a family whose conversation turned entirely on the two married couples; the subject became so oppressive it made his head swim. "Nine o'clock—where are they now? What are they doing? Do they think of me at all?"

The lift was stuck at the third floor. The staircase smelled of cold food and disinfectant. Shrill voices and the clatter of crockery came through the chocolate-brown doors. Each family was parked in its little niche, with its joys and sorrows and passions, only a thin layer of cement separating it from the families to its right and left, and upstairs and downstairs, who had their own joys and sorrows and passions too, and cared nothing for those of their neighbours. A great mass of human lives cut up into cubes and stacked neatly in a box.

When he reached the sixth-floor landing, Gérard was so breathless that he had to lean against the lift cage.

A sewing machine was clattering away with a muffled sound in the silence of the Lequesnes' flat. When Gérard rang the bell the sewing machine stopped. Doors were opened and closed again; he heard hurried footsteps, and an unfamiliar voice saying, "It's all right, I'll go." The door opened.

A woman's face, chalky white and thin, with anxious eyes, appeared in the doorway. This must be Lequesne's mother, although he had never introduced Gérard to her.

"Oh, did you want to see Julien? Wait a minute!"

She called Julien. Again, doors opened and closed, and footsteps approached.

"Here he is." The woman went away, slippers flapping.

"Hullo, Fonsèque." Lequesne let him into the hall, which was narrow and passage-like, with grey wallpaper. It was cluttered with trunks, and the sewing machine, now abandoned, was enthroned in one corner.

"I know you weren't expecting me," said Gérard. "Is it a bad moment?"

"No, no!"

Lequesne was wearing black trousers and an olive-green sweater. He did, in fact, seem rather put out by Gérard's visit. He attempted a smile, and glanced at the door on the right through which his mother had vanished. Scraps of fabric and white thread littered the floor.

"I'm awfully sorry," he added, "but we can't go into my room—my mother needs it for her dressmaking. Shall we go out for a drink? There's a café quite close. I'll just get my jacket on and be back."

Once in the café he relaxed a little, and talked about his law studies and his future plans. "I've been offered a job as French tutor, with an English family living in London. My mother wants me to take it, but of course it would interrupt my studies."

"You know, you've got some sense after all, under all that sporting mystical stuff of yours!"

"Sporting mystical stuff?"

"Divine tennis matches and all that!"

Lequesne laughed quietly. When he laughed, his eyes deepened in colour to the shade of some strong liquor, and his healthy young teeth shone in his unshaven face.

"Not annoyed with me for that theory, are you?"

"No, no!" said Gérard. "I just think it's a hopeless one. A warrant for loneliness and weakness."

"I don't know what you mean."

"Oh yes, you do!" said Gérard. "Before Christianity took hold, man trusted man! Within the tribe, the strong helped the weak. Everyone developed his own talents for the good of the community. But then they were told, 'Actually, you're on your own. Your neighbours mean nothing to you and you mean nothing to them, except through the medium of God.' So the shortest way from heart to heart was not a straight line any more, but a dotted line, with God intervening. Intermediaries should be abolished in morality as in industry!"

"There's always prayer."

"Yes, well, that's one remedy for loneliness. Christianity, like any quack doctor, creates both the sickness and the cure! Here's the microbe and here's the medicine for it. But we all have the microbe in us, and the medicine's only within the reach of a few. Hence all the trouble. Man must learn how to be proud, decisive and bold again. 'While your morality hung over my head, I was like a suffocating man,' said Nietzsche. We have been made weak, we have been made anxious, we have been condemned to a perpetual childhood. We're tied for ever to the Lord's apron strings. For centuries, we've been brought up wrapped in the cottonwool of Christianity. Let's have some fresh air! 'They say the fight is long and bloody over there . . .' That was well said by Verlaine! You're no warrior in the Nietzschean sense, Lequesne."

"That sort of warrior's cut out to be a victim!"

"What does it matter? I'd rather be a defeated man than one who makes no effort. Oh, by the way, I have the start of my Essay here—perhaps you'd like to read it?"

Lequesne took the sheets of paper Gérard was offering him and glanced through the first few lines, his face falling.

Fonsèque laughed, rubbing his long, limp hands together. "Well, the text *is* rather shocking—but so it should be. I decided I must strike home 'to establish in them, by the sweat of their brows, the empire of the Will', as Jouffroy says."

61

"The empire of *your* will, you mean!" Lequesne remarked.

He had started to read again. Gérard was watching his face; it took on a triangular shape in the artificial lighting from above. Paul Aucoc would have informed them it was like an El Greco. (He had visited many art galleries abroad.) If Luce could have seen Lequesne now, Gérard felt sure she would have admired his face, shadowed at temples and chin, with deep eye sockets; would have been struck by the intelligent, dark, lively expression of his eyes themselves behind their long, girlish lashes. She already liked him, anyway. At Elisabeth's wedding, Gérard had seen a sort of playful tenderness in her eyes and voice, and he could easily guess the cause of it. But where another man would have seized his chance, Lequesne had beaten a retreat. Oh, how he would like his friend to court Luce, all the same: deliver her from her husband, shatter the absurdity of her marriage to Aucoc for good! And this wish of his seemed to him proof positive of his own unselfishness. How could he be accused of egotism when he wanted his sister to leave her husband, not to come back home, but to live with a young man who was good enough for her? He was acting in her own interests, pursuing her own happiness for her. And yet some scruple, he could not have said just what, prevented him from deceiving himself entirely.

He rose to his feet. "Mind if I leave you for a moment? I have to make a telephone call."

The telephone kiosk was at the back of the café. Gérard closed the glass door behind him. The place still smelled disturbingly of the perfume of a woman who had been in there telephoning before him. Through the glass panes, he saw Lequesne busy reading his manuscript. He picked up the receiver, dialled a number, and waited.

"Hullo? Wagram 8458? Is that you, Luce? Gérard here. I'm out in a café with Lequesne—we've nothing special to do this evening, can we drop in and see you?"

When he put the receiver down, his mouth was twisted in a wily smile. He must get Luce and Lequesne face to face: then he could evaluate his friend's chances better. A trial step.

Later, he could decide if there was any future in taking things further.

Beyond the glass, at the far end of the room, Lequesne went on turning the pages of the manuscript, unaware of the trap being set. Gérard felt the excited pleasure of the chase at the sight of him. Safe in his glass cage, he gloated quietly over his prey.

At last he came out and went back to the table. "Lequesne, I was supposed to go and see Luce this evening," he said. "I've just telephoned to say I was with you, and she'd like us both to go along. We can be at her place in quarter of an hour if we take a taxi."

He stopped, watching his friend. A change had come over the young man's face. His eyes rounded in childlike astonishment; his lips relaxed.

"Oh . . . I won't go," he muttered.

"Why not?"

"I don't really want to see your sister again."

"You didn't mind seeing her at Elisabeth's wedding!"

"That wasn't the same."

"What on earth do you mean?"

"Well, there was a whole crowd of people there."

Gérard laughed. "Oh, so it's the idea of being alone with her that scares you? Don't worry—her husband will be around!"

Lequesne bowed his head. "Don't laugh at me, Gérard. You had no right to beg an invitation for me!"

Gérard immediately protested his innocence: Luce herself had insisted on Lequesne's coming round. It was only natural; she had a liking for him, and he himself was the only one who had failed to notice it. She would be disappointed if he didn't go. She would wonder why. Perhaps she would *guess* why! That could be very dangerous. As he spoke, Gérard watched his friend's face, seeing in it the promise of defeat and acquiescence.

"Of course, you can do as you like, but it would be rude to refuse the invitation . . . and a pity, too!"

63

Lequesne ran a finger over his cheeks. "I haven't shaved."

Was that all he could find to say? Vigneral would have expressed himself no differently! Gérard remembered his conversation with Lequesne on Luce's wedding day, when his friend visited him. He had been impressed by Lequesne then, by his fine-drawn face and the assurance of his ideas. But it seemed a love affair was enough to show him in a less advantageous light. They were all the same! "Oh women, show me the child in the man!"—thus spake Zarathustra.

"Anyway, it's getting late," objected the unfortunate young man.

But Fonsèque was already taking down his hat and coat. Lequesne obediently rose to his feet.

*   *   *

The maid showed them into a large and formal room, its ceiling bright with concealed lighting. The flowing curtains were steel-grey.

"Madame will be just a moment—would you wait?"

Modern furniture, its surface as shiny as the bodywork of a motor car, was arranged along the walls. The floor was covered with an off-white carpet, like a piece of uncooked pastry. The textured wall-covering was the colour of sawdust, and the walls were hung with pallid pictures of street corners and railway lines in the rain. A little white dog was asleep on a brandy-coloured cushion. The room might have come straight from the exhibition area of some big store, and seemed to be waiting for the arrival of wax dummies; it was uninhabited, uninhabitable, dead.

The two young men did not have time to sit down before the door behind them opened and Luce came in, followed by Paul Aucoc.

"Oh, we've kept you waiting! I'm so sorry—do sit down!"

She was playing the part of hostess with studied detachment, and was visibly proud of her status as a married woman, of her apartment, her money and her social graces.

"What a good idea of yours to phone us! The one evening of

64

the week when we're free, too!"

"Don't forget, darling, we're going to supper with the Prouvelat-Duteilles!"

"Yes, but not till later, darling! We've got plenty of time yet!"

"I say, do you know Lequesne really admires your interior decoration here?" said Gérard. "He was just telling me so when you came in!"

Startled by this piece of fiction, Lequesne looked at Gérard, but his friend was not smiling.

"Oh, do you?" cried Luce. "It was Paul who designed it."

"Well, I sketched out the plans," said Paul. "You see, I set great store by tones and spatial relations. It was a pity I couldn't get the exact shades I was after. I'd meant the lining of the curtains to be shrimp-pink, but the shop could only provide pale salmon!"

"What a fuss he made about it, too!" said Luce.

She insisted on showing them the other rooms in the apartment because "it all added up to a whole". The three men followed her as she walked down the corridor, graceful and slender, looking as if she were strolling along a beach.

"This is Paul's study . . . here's our bedroom . . ."

When they were back in the drawing room, Lequesne looked exhausted, as if he had been walking for a long time, and along rough roads. Gérard felt irritated by his unenterprising melancholy. This visit ought to have roused the young man to jealousy! Such a sense of carnality about the place, of the life of a married couple! What more did he need to stimulate him to action? Wasn't it enough for him to see Luce glued to her plump husband's side, steering her way from room to room, showing him all the compartments of her private life, one by one, rubbing his nose in the pleasures he had missed? Couldn't he see what his chances must be, compared to that fat, pretentious fool?

The conversation was going rather stickily. "Oh, Monsieur Lequesne, don't you think life in Paris is intolerable? Paul and I are in the most terrible state of nerves! All the hustle and bustle! The traffic! The rat-race! Do you go out much in the evening?"

"Hardly at all, Madame."

"How lucky you are! A free evening is quite a rarity for us! And it's a long time until Christmas! I expect you're going away for the Christmas holiday?"

"Well, no, not for Christmas—but I might be going away before that, for longer than the holiday. A family in England have offered me a job as a tutor, to teach French . . ."

"Hang on!" exclaimed Gérard. "Didn't you tell me just now you were going to turn it down?"

"I hadn't really made up my mind."

"I love England!" stated Paul. "Not for its historic monuments, not for its landscapes—for the exquisite quality of the English light! The visibility blurred, as if veiled by muslin! You can explain the whole of British literature and art if you start from that observation."

"You're going away for so long? What a pity!" said Luce. "It would have been nice if you could have come to spend a weekend at *Les Trembles*—that's my parents-in-law's place in the country. We're inviting several friends there in early November—you know, you'd have been very welcome!"

Lequesne turned his eyes on her with a serious, keen, surprised expression in them.

"Don't worry, Luce, he hasn't left yet!" said Gérard.

He rose to his feet and strolled away, to give himself a better vantage point from which to view the three people whose lives he wanted to bend to his own liking: Aucoc, showing off, self-important, dandified, revoltingly proprietorial; Luce twittering away at her guest like a bird in spring. As for Lequesne, he was sitting with his feet tucked under his chair, pale-faced and frowning, looking like someone charged with an offence, undergoing examination by the magistrate. The little white dog had come over to the unfortunate man and was sniffing hard at his trouser turn-ups and his shoes. Annoyed by its persistence, Lequesne tried to push its inquiring muzzle away with his hand, but to no avail.

66

"Jenny's taken a liking to you!" said Luce, attempting to put him at his ease.

He flushed. No doubt, thought Gérard, he was overcome by a sense of his poor chances of pleasing such a woman: surrounded by valuable things, leisured, elegant, capricious and not very intelligent. Gérard himself was beginning to think his undertaking a crazy one. In fact, the whole manoeuvre seemed so puerile he was surprised he had ever expected anything to come of it. Taking Lequesne to see the Aucocs with him made no difference to anything.

"I really must be going," said Lequesne, rather feebly. "It's getting late, and you have to go out."

"Yes, it's time we were off too," said Paul. "Half past seven—the Prouvelat-Duteilles are expecting us at eight."

"Oh, darling, couldn't you go on your own?" said Luce. "I do feel so tired! You can say I've got a headache, and Gérard will stay and keep me company."

When the door had closed behind Paul and Lequesne, Luce went away to put a housecoat on, and then came back to the drawing room, where her brother was waiting for her and teasing the dog. She seemed suddenly more vulnerable in her floating garment of pink crêpe.

He watched her sit down, take the dog on her lap and pet it gently.

"How funny he did look!" she said, abruptly.

He started, brought back to the business in hand. Although he knew perfectly well what she meant, he asked, "Who?"

"Why, Lequesne, of course!"

"That's hardly surprising."

"Why?"

"Oh, come on, don't act all innocent!"

"I can assure you *I* don't know why!"

He pushed his glasses up on his forehead, rubbed the top of this nose, and said in even tones, "Well, you certainly beat your own record!"

"Is he in some sort of trouble?"

"I'll say he is!"

"In love?"

"Now why, when a woman thinks of trouble, is love the first thing that occurs to her? Woman are so blinkered they can't see any farther!"

"He isn't in love, then?"

"Yes, he is."

"And *she* doesn't love *him*?"

"Can one ever know?"

"You mean he daren't tell her?"

"No."

"Who is she?"

"You!"

She seemed amazed. "Good gracious—are you mad?" she whispered.

"*He* is?"

"Did he tell you all this himself?"

"He talks of nothing else."

She burst into artificial laughter, throwing her pretty hands up in the air and then clasping them. "Oh, what a story! How funny! Oh dear, poor thing! No, no, it's quite impossible! I mean, if I'd noticed any such thing before my marriage . . . but honestly, I'd never have believed it! At least, I wouldn't have thought he was *so* much in love! And is he upset about it?"

The avidity with which she put that question!

"Don't worry, he's badly upset."

"But that's dreadful! Did he ask you to bring him here this evening?"

"No."

"So it was your idea?"

"Yes."

"Why ever did you do it?"

"Don't you think the best way to discourage a suitor is to show him the woman he loves, deeply in love with someone else? Now he's seen the pair of you living in perfect harmony. A model marriage. An indestructible union, able to withstand

68

any trial! He's realized he was an intruder, it was no use staring at the warmth of your conjugal felicity from outside, you were lost to him, lost to all sense of adventure . . ."

"Thank you very much!"

"What have I said! Nothing unflattering, surely?"

"No . . . but it's the way you put things!"

He did not reply to this. So he'd gauged it right! Luce did not like to think *he* thought her unable to carry on a successful flirtation.

"Gérard, what should I do?" she asked.

"Well, there are two alternatives: either you refuse ever to see him again—"

"Do you think that would be good tactics?"

He smiled. "Well, it would be a bit brutal, but quite justifiable. Either you do that, or you pretend you don't know how he feels, you invite him here as if it were a perfectly natural thing to do, and you let familiarity breed contempt."

"That would be better, don't you think?"

"It calls for a good deal of skill."

"I dare say! But I wouldn't want to hurt your friend—I like him so much, and it's all so sad!"

Gérard made haste to assure her that Lequesne was really a most talented young man, with a brilliant career ahead of him if he were to devote himself to literature. At the moment he wrote only verse, and he had not published anything so far.

"Oh, I'd love to read his poetry! Do you think he'd show it to me?"

"Perhaps, but you wouldn't understand it!"

"Want to bet?"

"Bet on what?"

"Bet I do understand it!"

Gérard shrugged his shoulders. "You still haven't given me *Le Meurtre de Monsieur Nolle* back," he remarked.

"I don't see the connection!"

"There isn't any—that's my point!"

"Oh, I wish you wouldn't talk in riddles. It's really infuriating!"

Irritated, she snapped her fingers, and the little dog jumped off her lap and made for the cushion, wagging its tail.

"That animal is a true philosopher," said Gérard.

"Why?"

"When it sees a woman getting upset, it decides to beat a prudent retreat and go to sleep in a corner—and I'm going to follow its example!"

"I am not getting upset!"

"Just look at yourself in the glass!"

"Well, suppose I *am* upset, isn't all this business enough to upset anyone?"

"All what business?"

"About Lequesne! I mean, what you've told me—it *is* upsetting!"

"Very likely, for him."

She stretched her long, graceful arms, narrowed her eyes, swelled her breast, dove-like, and cooed languorously, "Oh, my goodness me, how very strange! What strange creatures men are . . . how strange life is!"

"I am sure you're about to say something extremely profound!" said Gérard. "It's time I went home—but listen, I must beg you not to repeat this conversation to Paul! It would be tactless, and rather unkind."

"What on earth are you thinking of? Of course this will be a secret between us . . . Gérard, suppose he writes to me?"

"Oh, I don't think he'll go to such lengths. He's not taken leave of his senses entirely!"

"I'm not so sure of that," she said.

II

To the sound of mild laughter and a little fluttering of papers, the predominantly female audience of the Ecole du Louvre lectures made its way quickly to the exit. Marie-Claude crossed the threshold, and could not help exclaiming, "Vigneral!"

He was standing in a corner of the inner courtyard, scanning the talkative, shallow, painted faces streaming out through the doorway to an accompaniment of high heels clattering. On hearing his name, he turned his head and saw Marie-Claude.

"What are you doing here?" she asked.

He smiled, standing very tall in front of her, his raincoat open to show an unbuttoned jacket; he was not wearing a waistcoat today. He had a briefcase under his right arm, while his left hand held a rolled-up felt hat. His untidy fair hair was blowing in the wind.

"I was waiting for you," he said simply.

"Just me—or someone else?"

"No, just you! You see I'd had about enough of trying to sell carbon paper to people who don't want it, and it was five-fifteen, and I found myself in the rue de Rivoli. Well, I remembered you go to lectures here, so I thought I'd see if I could meet you on your way out."

She looked at him, surprised. "You were lucky, then, because I come out at a different time every day, and it's all rather complicated . . . but what on earth made you suddenly do that?" She was speaking rather fast and breathlessly, in a jerky voice. She blushed when two girls who had been sitting beside her in the lecture turned after passing them, and looked back. "Let's go, then!" she said.

"Yes, let's! I was feeling really lost among all those girls . . . there are some pretty ones there, though! Well—

71

would you like to go and have tea in a little place I know? It's quite close."

It really was a little place, with a low ceiling, walls panelled in pale wood, bottle-glass in the windows, and English prints on the walls. There were not many customers, and they sat at a corner table by the window.

Marie-Claude was delighted with this little adventure. The mere fact that Vigneral, her brother's friend, had gone out of his way to have a chat with her struck her as extremely flattering. (Did he think she was intelligent, then, or amusing, or pretty?) She wished she was more smartly dressed. She wasn't wearing any face-powder, and her long-sleeved grey sweater, which he had seen before, had a spot of ink on its cuff. Her hands were unmanicured, her hair was untidy. At this very moment he was looking at her sweater and her hands and her hair, with an odd smile.

"Well, I'm glad to see you've given up those badges!" he said.

How self-confident he was! Marie-Claude did not care for this sally. "I didn't remember to put them on, that's all," she muttered. "I won't forget tomorrow."

He laughed merrily and shook his head. "Wonderful! Wonderful! I'm exhausted, my little Marie-Claude. I've been chasing about all day for nothing. See my sales book? Two boxes of carbon paper, six typewriter ribbons, and that's all. It's only too clear that if my parents didn't give me a bit of help I could never make ends meet, even on a bachelor's budget! Talk about humiliating!"

His voice sounded over-loud in this quiet room, accustomed to the murmuring of elderly ladies of leisure and decorous married couples. As he talked, he poured the tea with a large man's clumsy gestures. It amused her to see him employ unnecessary force in handling the tiny china teapot, which had a spout shaped like the calyx of a flower. What she liked about him was his forthright nature, a sort of clumsy but healthy gaiety. How could Gérard disparage him? She wanted him to go on talking about his day's work, his weariness, his

72

other troubles. "Why don't you look for a different job?" she asked.

"Because I'm no good at anything! I can't stand the thought of sitting in an office. In my line of work, at least I'm on the move, I see people, I try to do them down, and I feel I'm alive!"

"You think being alive means doing people down?"

"So does everyone else! Life would be very boring if we weren't all doing each other down! There's a quotation from what's-his-name, La Fontaine: 'Life is a comedy in a hundred acts, its stage the universe . . .'"

"You'd better leave the quotations to Gérard!"

"Now, take a man and a woman in love. The more in love they are, the more they're doing each other down. And the more they do each other down, the more they love each other. When *you* get married . . ."

She started; she didn't like it when anyone alluded to her marrying. "Can't you talk about something else?" she said. But then, why did she add (as she immediately did), "Anyway, I've no intention of getting married!" As if she were afraid he might indeed change the subject.

"Oh, come on, that line's so old it isn't even funny any more!" he said. "Every girl I know—"

She was ruffled. "I don't want to hear about every girl you know!"

He took her hand in a firm clasp. "Here, hang on!" he said in a humorous tone. "Don't let's get carried away!"

What *was* the matter with her? She wished she hadn't said that! She had made herself look ridiculous. He must think her silly and bad-tempered. She drank her tea, gulping it down, while he looked at her with a smile. Oh, I hope he doesn't go on about it, she thought. And he did not.

She began talking about Gérard with an assumed lack of selfconsciousness. Gérard was working on another translation. Gérard had advised her to read Proust "and make notes". He was getting on with his essay on Evil, but had refused to let her see it, saying it was dynamite. Vigneral listened with a feeling of boredom. Why did she feel impelled to carry on about everything her brother did? He was vaguely troubled by the admiration for Gérard he could sense in what she said. "Are you very fond of Gérard?" he asked.

"What a question! Of course I am!"

"I suppose he's a real friend to you; you confide in him—"

"Oh no!"

"Why not?"

"I'd never dare tell him the things I think!"

"Wouldn't he understand?"

"I don't think so."

"Don't you think he's a little . . . well, peculiar?"

"He's awfully clever!"

"Yes, I'm sure, but don't you feel he's somehow different from other people?"

"Good for him if he is!"

Was she really a fool, or was she trying to discourage any more conversation? She was drinking her tea again, eyes half-closed, cheeks flushed, and when she raised her head, her childish lips were wet.

Vigneral looked at her wan little face with its emerald eyes, her slender body, the firm, high breasts straining the grey wool of her sweater. He also noticed the inkspot on its cuff, which was beginning to unravel. Just a child, not even a pretty one really. Suppose they met any people he knew in the street? Much use it would be telling them later on that this insignificant-looking girl was only a friend—they wouldn't believe him! They would spread the rumour that he had a seventeen-year-old mistress, commonplace, badly dressed and shy. He was very anxious for others to admire a woman who was with him. He thought of Tina's dark, pointed mischievous face with its beautiful and skilful lips. Marie-Claude's face seemed even less attractive by comparison. As if she had guessed what he was thinking, she got out a compact and powdered it, with small, nervous, patting gestures.

"Don't stare at me!" she said, and added, "Goodness, you might have told me my nose was shining!"

74

This sounded like a remark Luce had made in front of her, and which she was now parroting.

It had been unwise to go and meet her from her lecture. At the very least, she must be thinking he'd fallen in love with her. Girls of seventeen can find material for a whole novel in what was merely a polite gesture. He lit a cigarette. "I won't offer you one," he said.

"Why not? I'd like one!"

"Smoking now, are you?"

"I've been smoking for ages!"

He knew she had been doing no such thing, and was only trying to impress him with her sophistication. After a few puffs, she began coughing. "My goodness, they're strong!"

He did not reply; he was feeling bored, and wanted to leave. He took out a coin and tapped it on the edge of his saucer.

"Oh, is it getting late?" Marie-Claude asked.

"I really don't know," he said calmly, and was then immediately sorry for the boorishness of this remark. She turned her sad little face away from him. He had not noticed the spot near her mouth before, or the powder accumulated beside her nostrils. These details were both pathetic and endearing. To make up for his rudeness, he suggested seeing her home.

"Oh, no thank you," she said quickly. "I'd rather go home alone."

"You're not angry, are you?"

"What for?"

Yes, what for, indeed? They had both risen to their feet; Vigneral helped Marie-Claude on with her coat. She smelled healthily of skin cream.

When she had left, he stayed in the café for some time, musing by the dark window panes. This was all absurd! He felt annoyed with himself. He felt annoyed with her. And when he had paid the bill, he had not got enough money left to spend the evening in the Toc-Toc Bar.

*   *   *

Gérard came into his mother's room and sat down beside her. She was knitting.

"She's not back yet," he said.

"It's only twenty to seven."

"But her lecture finished at five-thirty!"

"She may have gone to see a girl friend."

Mme Fonsèque had her head on one side, and laborious breathing, like an old woman's, came from her opened lips. A lock of grey hair had come adrift and was falling over her cheek.

Gérard begrudged her such calm, when he was so worried. "What's that you're knitting?" he asked, snappishly.

"A bed-jacket for Luce."

"She'll never wear it."

"Why not?"

When he was in a bad temper he felt this petty wish to hurt his mother, and yet he had deep affection for her: the affection of a grown and moody son. He was the kind of man, however, whose affection needs to be constantly stimulated: after every quarrel, he loved the poor woman more, with a faintly remorseful feeling, a sort of ill-tempered pity.

He shrugged his shoulders and took off his glasses, which were tiring him. His eyes looked small and stupid in his suddenly naked face.

"I'm worn out!" he said. "People think an office is the only place any real work gets done, but I know I get through more at home than any office workers! Donkey-work too, not much more interesting than theirs!"

This remark was aimed at his mother. The previous evening, she had been bewailing the fact that he had turned down a job the Aucocs had offered him in their salted-provisions business.

Mme Fonsèque sighed, and scratched her head with her knitting needle. "You'd better go and lie down for a while, Gérard. Why are you wearing that waistcoast over your pullover, dear? Do you feel cold?"

"Probably."

He rose and went over to the window; it was not raining, and a greyish mist blotted out the night.

The Telliers had dined with them last night. Elisabeth seemed to be immersed in that smug contentment that makes other woman say, "Ah, she needed a man!" Her husband's eyes dwelt constantly on her as he ate. Gérard felt ill at ease facing the couple. He was not so much of a brother as before. He could not snub his sister or make fun of her as he used to. When he criticized her hat, saying it was "as full of flowers as a railway-station garden", he noticed the expression of annoyance on his mother's face and the curious look on Tellier's, the look of someone whose rights are being infringed, of the man in occupation thinking: why is *he* poking his nose in? Then there was Luce. She had promised to invite Gérard and Lequesne out into the country, but nothing more had been heard from her since! Would he have to remind her of her promise? And Marie-Claude still wasn't home! His anger grew, feeding on first one and then another of his sisters. He was in a general state of anxiety, like those yapping dogs one sees perched on laundry vans and barking at passers-by, their paws buried among the bundles of washing.

He moved away from the window and paced about the room, bad-tempered, bored, and at a loose end. Then he stopped in front of his mother. "I'll go to the station and wait for her," he said.

The road was being mended at the corner of the rue Saint-Antoine, and ragged old women and squalid girls came to scavenge the wooden paving blocks split up by the labourers's picks. Four red lights marked off the now deserted site, and here they bent and straightened up again, looking absurd and malevolent as they stuffed their booty into baskets. One girl was filling an old pram with sand. Gérard skirted his way round them, and was back on the busy pavement that ran past the shops. He did not like this noisy, busy street, lined with its ramparts of victuals. The sight of such a lavish display of food

77

made him feel quite sick. Those blocks of sickly yellow butter, perfunctorily veiled in muslin! Those pale-bellied fish flung down on branches of evergreen! Those piled mounds of vegetables! Those monstrous mountains of meat, their great oval wounds no longer bleeding: a neat display of mutilated stumps on a white, clean and clinical background. A lorry had stopped in between two butchers' shops, and a hefty man, wearing a brown-spotted towel round his head like a turban, was hoisting a quarter of a bullock over his shoulder. Walking with knees bent, he carried it into the shop, where empty meat hooks awaited it. The enormous mass of flesh flopped against the man, clinging voluptuously close to him.

A crowd of housewives were jostling each other around the displays, like flies round a puddle of honey. They moved back and forth, chattering, their purses clutched to them, their heads full of mean little calculations, their eyes greedy. Amidst this distasteful smell of food, they were choosing something to stuff down their families that night. He felt their ugliness, their poverty, their scurrying, greedy, hen-like haste as a slap in the face. Where did his horrified dislike of common people come from? He was writing a book to instruct those who knew nothing of happiness in that subject, and here he was hating them! I can only work well when I'm angry, he thought.

Yet these horrible women had something in common with his sisters. They were *all* sisters under the skin, in the very essence of their minds. They were closer to Elisabeth, Luce and Marie-Claude than he would ever be!

He bumped into a young woman who turned and smiled at him. She was pale and looked dishevelled in the glaring light of the shops. He could follow her, speak to her. But why? Could love bring about the fusion of which he dreamed? He had once thought so, thought it would be good not to be alone any more, to forget oneself, to breathe more easily for a while, laying down one's own burden. But no. Amorous communing was a snare and a delusion. A spark of spiritual exaltation becomes more earthy, implants itself in the flesh,

78

rises to the point of irritation in one particular organ of that flesh—and once the spasm is discharged, he thought, nothing is left but a weary and rather comic sense of exhaustion. "Alas, my desire is vain. Where is the hope of unity?" writes Tagore. Life was only butchery, commerce, eating and sleeping . . .

He reached the exit from the underground station. A newspaper vendor was shouting tonelessly, "*Paris-Soir! L'Intran!*" Near his poster, an elderly woman was adjusting her stocking, skirt hoisted up. The seductive posture was in ludicrous contrast with her fat legs, swollen by varicose veins, and her face, wrinkled as an old glove.

At regular intervals, the mouth of the Métro opened and spewed forth a crowd of people. The idea that Marie-Claude would soon come towards him, carried along on this human tide, rather revolted him. Marie-Claude, pressed close to all those bellies and thighs and shoulders, surrounded by that disgusting smell of meat on the hoof! Why was she late? Perhaps she had felt ill during the lecture. She often told him the lecture hall was too hot. Perhaps she had been run over by a car. He went over all possible reasons for major anxiety in his mind, without believing in them very much.

He was cold. He was probably catching a cold tonight, just as he had on the eve of Luce's wedding. "Oh, what bad luck!" his mother had said, and Luce came to see him before going to her maiden bed for the very last time, her face covered with vaseline, a hairnet imprisoning the flame of her hair. She smelled of soap and clean skin.

At twenty past seven, Marie-Claude found her brother standing on the pavement, collar turned up, hat well down over his ears.

"Where've you been?" he asked.

"Having tea with a friend."

"What friend?"

"Totote. Totote Rouchez. Don't you know her?"

No, he did not know Totote Rouchez, not that it mattered. He walked home beside his sister, relieved and tired. The

79

night air was scented with frost, petrol fumes, and smoke. He held the girl's arm tight and did not speak, only looked at her with a mixture of anxiety and delight, as if he had nearly lost her.

III

Les Trembles, the Aucocs' villa, was a heavy, grey stone building, low-roofed and with large windows, surrounded by tall, dark trees.

Luce came out on the front steps to welcome Gérard. "Lequesne's already arrived," she said, in a rush, "but you know, it really wasn't my idea to invite him!"

"Whose was it, then?"

"Paul's! Paul likes him—and in the circumstances I could hardly object! It would have looked suspicious."

"You did quite right."

"Yes, I did, didn't I?" She was very pleased with herself.

In the huge ground-floor drawing room, cluttered with furniture upholstered in severe-looking tapestry work, Elisabeth, Joseph Tellier and Lequesne were sitting round in a semi-circle making polite conversation to the elder Aucocs. Paul stood behind the guests, face smooth and shiny as a bun, hair slicked down, the knot of his tie jutting, watching fondly over this scene with a melting blue eye.

"You ought to stand at the next cantonal elections," Tellier was saying.

"Well—it's not impossible that I may be tempted!" said M. Aucoc senior. "We need some fresh points of view in politics! Myself, I am firmly rooted in French soil, but my patriotism is not blind. One must hold one's head high, yet still be able to see one's feet. I know that young people aren't always of that opinion—" here he shook hands with Gérard without interrupting his speech—"and will admit of no compromises. But we older folk, Monsieur Tellier, we are aware that truth is to be found half-way up the hillside. Which is why I wanted to call this house *Truth*, but my wife didn't care for it!"

"Just think of the jokes!" said Mme Aucoc. "*Truth* to let! *Truth* is up for sale!"

"*Truth* would never have been for sale or to let within my lifetime!" Aucoc raised a finger to point at the ceiling: corseted, bombastic and turgid as he was, he yet had a certain grandeur about him.

"Did you have a good journey, Gérard?" asked Mme Aucoc. "We're some way from Paris here, of course—but it really is so pleasant to leave all the noise and bustle behind and immerse oneself in fresh air, silence and greenery!"

This was obviously a favourite saying of her husband's, and Mme Aucoc savoured every word of it like some choice delicacy.

She was so sorry to hear that Marie-Claude had stayed at home to write up her lecture notes, and Mme Fonsèque had not wanted to leave her on her own, but she did hope Gérard and Lequesne would stay until Tuesday! As for the Telliers, they would be going back by coach on Monday morning, since they were both at work on Mondays.

"I like people to feel at home in my house! I really want them to forget all about me! Madame de Fauchois often used to tell me she automatically got her key out when she reached my door, she felt so much as if it were her own home! Don't you think that's the best compliment anyone can pay the mistress of a house?"

She was cooing, her glances sugary, one finger patting the curls that covered her head like little pastry shapes.

"Luce, why don't you show your brother and his friend the garden?" she went on. "Monsieur Tellier and Elisabeth saw it this morning—they'll stay here and keep us company. But do put a coat on! It's cold outside."

Gérard looked at Lequesne, who had risen, and was following Luce with his eyes. His face wore an expression of glowing ardour that made him look younger. All because he had been invited here for the weekend and his hopes were reviving! How farcical! And yet, thought Gérard, that's exactly what I wanted.

They went out of doors. Luce and Lequesne walked in front, with Gérard and Paul Aucoc following close behind them. But for his own amusement, Gérard progressively slowed his pace. While he talked to Paul, he kept one ear attuned to the small talk being exchanged by the young couple ahead of them.

"I've never been any good at recognizing garden plants— trees and herbs and vegetables! What are those?" Luce was asking.

"Cabbages," Lequesne told her. "And those are beetroot, and that's parsley. I say, look at the trunk of that tree! Looks as if a goat's been chewing it. Those two ragged edges of bark will have to be grafted together again."

"How—with bits of wood?"

"You use one-year-old shoots of the same species as the damaged tree." He had picked up a dead branch lying on the ground and was switching his leg with it. "You make diagonal cuts at the ends and insert them under the bark, and then you cover the whole area with grafting wax. Ask the gardener to let you watch him do it—it's an interesting operation."

He broke the branch and tossed the pieces away.

"What an extraordinary person you are! How do you come to know all this?"

"Oh, I lived in the country as a child."

Gérard stopped, pretending he had to tie his shoe. When he straightened up, the couple were some way off, and he could not make their words out any more.

Luce walked with a springy step, adapted to strolling in gardens. (An article in her favourite fashion magazine the previous week had described the ways in which a modern young woman, aiming to be attractive, should suit her style of movement to the nature of the terrain.) She had picked a blade of grass and was sucking it, thus allowing a glimpse of her sharp teeth. Even though the sun was not shining, she felt she was looking very pretty. Lequesne had good reason to be in love with her. Of course, if he had declared his love she would have put him in his place—but a little unspoken adoration was very pleasant. In a light-hearted tone, she teased him.

"I didn't think you liked fresh air and the countryside! I thought you were one of Gérard's sort! You keep your feelings to yourself, don't you?"

"Yes."

She felt a little thrill of anticipatory pleasure. Here we go, she thought.

"Too shy to express them?"

"Too prudent."

"Oh, you shouldn't be prudent! I don't like prudent men! One should be able to throw oneself deliberately into adventure!"

"I do—but I choose my adventures."

"Using your reason?"

"No."

"Your instinct?"

"I don't like the word."

"But the thing itself is so nice!" She was pleased with this reply. She tilted her head in a drowsy attitude, and smiled softly. Lequesne turned his face towards her: it was thin and pale, with large dark eyes that slanted towards the temples. Luce thought he looked "interesting", seen in three-quarter profile with his head bent. Men don't pay enough attention to the way they present themselves, she thought; they achieve good looks only by chance, and almost without noticing.

"Gérard tells me you write poetry," she went on.

He blushed, lowering his eyelids. "Yes . . . yes, I do."

"What sort of poetry?"

She did not in the least mind discussing literature with a young man who was better educated than herself, and whose competence even Gérard acknowledged. She had, to a very high degree, the feminine ability of saying anything to anyone, on any subject, with the conviction that she was dazzling her hearers by the aptness of her comments.

"Oh—about everything and nothing. Short poems on the sadness of life; other, very long poems about—well, hands, or the whistle of a train in the night, or . . ."

"Recite me the poems about the whistle of a train in the

84

night!"

He began to laugh, shaking his head. He was no longer in three-quarter profile, and she felt sorry.

"I've forgotten them!" he said. "Anyway, they weren't any good."

"Don't you write any poems about women?"

"Yes, of course."

"I wish someone would write poems about me!"

"That would not be very difficult."

"Wouldn't you like to try?"

"I already have," he said quietly.

She clapped her hands. "Oh, do say them to me!"

"I tore them up."

"Why?"

"They didn't give a very good idea of you."

"Will you write some more?"

They were standing side by side, gazing intently at each other.

"Yes, I will. I promise!" he murmured.

"Oh, and what's *that* tree, Monsieur Lequesne? An apple or a cherry?" she suddenly inquired in formal tones.

He jumped. Gérard and Paul were fast approaching, striding towards them.

After dinner, they went into the drawing room for liqueurs. M. Aucoc senior was still holding forth, while Tellier, weary and relaxed, listened without even trying to reply.

"Our financial system needs an infusion of new blood. The budget of the State is not properly balanced."

Mme Aucoc, Elisabeth and Luce were discussing clothes, headaches, good works. Gérard offered Paul a game of chess, the winner to play Lequesne.

They went into a tiny, overheated smoking room, cluttered with low chairs, apparently built to accommodate kangaroos, and small, vaguely Arab tables inlaid with mother-of-pearl. Oriental rugs hung on the walls. There were two embossed brass bowls on tripods either side of a divan. The Berger lamp

85

that had just been put out had left a fresh, sharpish odour in the room. The front steps of the house were visible through the French window, and were lit by a concealed lantern. Beyond them, the garden lay in darkness, with a glimmer of grey where the path must begin. The young men could hear the conversation coming from the next room, and the maid's footsteps upstairs on the floor above.

Seated at the chess board, Gérard and Paul were thinking hard, expressions of deep concentration on their faces, before every move. Lequesne was standing with a glass of cognac in his hand, and seemed to be following the game, but in fact his attention was entirely directed to picking out one particular voice from those in the room next door: a voice whose least utterance affected him. Having parried a tricky gambit, Gérard glanced at his friend. He loves her, he thought, he's hanging on her every word! Ready for any sort of folly! And she feels it too; he's gaining a strange influence over her.

"Your move Gérard."

He put out a hesitant hand above the decimated ranks of his pawns.

"Who's winning?"

Luce had pushed aside the curtain over the doorway, and was looking at the young men round the table.

"How do you expect us to tell you that before the game's over?" asked Paul.

"I don't like chess! It goes on too long, and the players always look so cross! I see you're not playing, Monsieur Lequesne?"

"I'm waiting for my turn."

"Then you'll be waiting all night! I'm going out to walk the dog—would you like to keep me company?"

He followed her, and soon Gérard saw their figures appear on top of the steps, go down them, and melt into the darkness.

"Check!" said Paul.

Gérard moved his queen, and Paul fell silent again, frowning and biting his lower lip thoughtfully.

He's looking at the trap I've set for him on the

86

chessboard—he doesn't suspect the one threatening him in real life, thought Gérard. His downfall is so close I really feel more pity than dislike for him.

The faltering notes of a waltz, picked out on the piano, brought him out of his thoughts. Mme Aucoc was playing in the next room.

"Schubert," said Paul.

"Perhaps."

By now, Luce and Lequesne must be sitting on that stone seat among the trees, surrounded by moist nocturnal scents. What were they saying? Were they holding hands yet? Were they kissing, in an ecstasy of pleasure and amazement? No, no, the affair was only just beginning . . . Gérard's heart beat fast, and he felt the blood throbbing in his tense fingertips. Paul, sitting opposite him, was fidgeting with the ivory chessman he held between finger and thumb.

"Oh, damn it all!" he said.

Poor fellow—he was so unsuspecting that Gérard suddenly felt like shouting the news of his deception out loud.

The piano music stopped; the renewed silence was unbearable. So was the melancholy that mingled so strangely with his elation. He rested his head in his hands, and suddenly felt he wanted to be able to weep, or to be alone with his books.

"Had enough, Gérard?"

"No, no!"

He pushed a pawn, with a careless finger. Mme Aucoc had started playing the piano again.

"Mozart," said Paul.

But Gérard was not listening to the music. He heard feet out on the steps. The hinges of the door squealed. Then he heard Luce's voice and her laugh in the drawing room. So they were back! In a few more minutes he would see them, and their eyes and words would surely give them away! He took out his handkerchief and mopped his eyes, cheeks and forehead; he was hot and sweating. The curtain rings rattled as they were pushed back along their rod.

"Oh, it's freezing outside!" said Luce.

She clasped her little hands with their red-painted nails, smiling with a look of sensuous confidence that told Gérard even more than he had hoped. Lequesne followed her into the room. He looked stunned, like a happy somnambulist.

"Haven't you two finished attacking each other's kings and queens yet?" said Luce. "You just watch how quickly *I* can settle the game!"

She made a playful lunge, as if to knock the chessboard over, but her husband caught her wrist in mid-air. With a quick, effusive impulse, she put her free arm round his neck, gave him a sudden kiss on the ear, whirled round and made her escape.

"Oh, I feel like really ruffling you up!" she cried. "Want to bet I sleep with the window open tonight?"

She uttered a trill of laughter, and Lequesne turned his eyes towards the dark window panes.

*　　*　　*

Was it the warmth of the sheets, or the unfamiliar smell of the room, or the muted ticking of the watch by his bedside that was keeping Gérard awake? Giving up the attempt to fall asleep, he forced himself to stop thinking. He felt that he must keep his reflections superficial if he were to preserve his peace of mind. Yet he was irresistibly attracted to probing the workings of his consciousness. He pictured the villa lost in the very middle of the night, surrounded by silence like rising water, inhabited by drowsy bodies breathing restlessly, dreaming. They approached, they touched, voices sought each other in the dark. Love? He had once tried to believe in the existence of a miraculously pure passion, but he would not let himself entertain the idea now. What was the good of deluding oneself any longer about the nature of the sentiment that impelled two hungry beings in one another's direction? "Marriage", "household", "husband", "other half"—he thought all the words relating to the situation were clumsy, ridiculous, inflated with bourgeois bombast and gross allusions to the carnal act. Love meant an anonymous room, hasty undressing, shirt coming out of underpants, dubious sock suspenders, damp petticoat, hairy or pimply bodies drawing towards each other, the garlicky smell of sweat, open-mouthed kisses, an awkward, jerky embrace, pathetic gasps of pleasure . . . by what despicable subterfuge, what pitiful complaisance, had this filth come to be endowed with all the attributes of grace? Why were the arts all in league to mask the animal face of Love? Poetry caused words they would never have uttered to spring from lovers' lips, music exalted the emotional disturbance of the impulse that brought them together, painting beautified the bovine expressions of their faces, sculpture polished the texture of their flesh—and generations of men and women pretended to believe in this lying image and recognize themselves in it, despite their diseases, the memories of their rutting, of their smell between the sheets! Surely it was the most widely accepted of conspiracies, the biggest camouflage exercise ever undertaken! But just try denouncing it, and the whole world, terrified at the thought of losing its illusions, will turn on you. "You don't understand anything about it . . . if you'd ever been in love . . . when you're in love . . ." He himself had never been in love. He never would be in love. That was certain. His relationships with women? There had been a mild flirtation with one of his sister's friends, when he was eighteen. They went for walks and visited the cinema together, and one day, for no particular reason stopped seeing each other. Then there was that incident in the brothel, the one he tried not to remember. That woman's stupid face, her soft, open painted mouth that smelled of her last meal. And then . . . well, encounters leading nowhere, conversations with a few double meanings . . . it amounted to nothing, really!

At first he had told himself he was undersexed, but now he thought otherwise. It was his extreme clarity of mind that denied him the pleasure of the senses. When other poeple's reason was swamped in disgusting ardours, his own struggled against obliteration, the dark night of the body, the madness of those lower regions. He had no trouble in overcoming animal desires, but another desire haunted him—to possess souls—and he could not deny himself that pleasure. He had thought that Lequesne at least understood him. But Lequesne was no better than the others, carefully as he cultivated his interior life. Luce only needed to call, and he would follow. The awkwardness of the situation did not frighten or discourage him, perhaps it even amused him. He was dabbling blithely in the waters of deception. To measure a man's true worth, thought Gérard, put him to bed! He'll shed his fine theories even before he sheds his clothes, revealing all the flaws of his spirit while his garments still veil the gross flaws of the body! No one passes the test!

At this moment, Gérard told himself, he is thinking of her and she is thinking of him, and it's my doing that they are both under this roof.

He hoisted himself up on his pillows. He was suffocating. Suddenly he felt afraid of the melancholy and malice he sensed in himself. But why should he feel unhappy? Wasn't he the one who had pushed them into each other's arms? Hadn't he hoped for and planned this very outcome?

The rain was running down the window panes, invisible in the dark, and the sound of it, like a talkative old woman's chatter, was there in the room with him. Suddenly he wondered if he were ill. No, his heart was beating regularly.

"There's nothing wrong with me," he murmured.

Luce was being passed from hand to hand. Lequesne was taking her away from Paul; someone else would take her away from Lequesne. How many men were there stalking her, sniffing the scent, tongues hanging out, waiting? Ah, the chase, the hunting of women! That was what was so horrible about it. It hardly mattered whether Luce thought of Lequesne rather than Paul or Vigneral in bed, when she looked into her mirror. How would he, Gérard, benefit if one man took another's place with her? He hated anyone who came between his sisters and himself. He did not merely want them to love him, he wanted to be the only object of their love. If they lavished a look or a thought on anyone else, he felt betrayed.

He remembered how, as a child, he detested anyone who spoke to his sisters and made them laugh. One day, when Elisabeth went out for a bicycle ride with a boy of her own age, he had shut himself up in a wardrobe, hoping to die of suffocation there. He had been found and laid on the drawing room sofa, and his mother wiped his face with a towel dipped in cold water. "But why did you hide there?" she asked. He would not answer.

Nobody would bend over him tonight to ask a soft-voiced question or wipe his hot forehead. Yet he still felt the same pain, so many years later, and the same people were the cause of it.

He lay motionless, crushed by this realization. And other memories came crowding in on him. That melancholy he had suddenly felt a few hours ago, when Luce and Lequesne came in from their walk. His fury when he saw certain intimate glances pass between Elisabeth and her husband. His fear of seeing Marie-Claude admire anyone, take an interest in any man! So that was it! He could no longer doubt it—he *did* no longer doubt it. His whole life had been lived in the fear of having his sisters torn from him, but anxiety can become as normal and permanent a state of mind as serenity, and it had taken this last incident, over Luce, to make him aware of his desperation. Now he was suffering intensely, with a sense of injured astonishment, or childish fear, and a wish to sob and cry out that constricted his throat. Pushing aside the undergrowth, he found a muddy puddle. He leaned over to look at the murky reflection in it, and trembled to recognize himself so clearly in that strange face.

It *is* me . . .

He fell back on his pillow, face bathed in sweat, temples throbbing.

What could he do? What happiness could he hope for; what

91

attitude should he adopt? Ought he to hope Lequesne would raise the siege? No, ridiculous. Better if the young man seized his chance—the main thing was to detach Luce from her husband. Then they'd see if the victor could defend his conquest. Say nothing, do nothing, let Fate take its course. But it was cruel to think he had been the architect of his own misfortune, set another face, another body between his sister and himself, one that might have remained in the shadows! He had encouraged their dawning love! He had made himself their accomplice!

Never mind, he thought, Lequesne must succeed; that's my last chance. It's my own happiness at stake . . .

Instinctively, he clasped his hands.

Outside, a branch cracked and fell. A door squeaked at the end of the corridor. Then all was silent again.

Gérard lit a cigarette. In the dim glass of the wardrobe mirror opposite, he could see the glowing tip move about in time to his gestures like a firefly. He put his whole mind to concentrating on the movements of that tiny light.

*   *   *

Gérard did not wake until nine o'clock. Rain-wet light was filtering in through the closed shutters. The room smelled slightly of plaster and furniture polish. A little clock in an open leather frame was ticking on the mantelpiece.

He got up, dressed quickly, and went out into the corridor. Lequesne's room was next to his. Gérard knocked on the door, but there was no reply. He was going to open it when the maid, who was just coming upstairs, stopped him.

"Oh, Monsieur Lequesne has left!" she said.

"What?"

"Yes, he left at half past seven this morning. He and Monsieur and Madame Tellier all caught the coach."

"Did he see anyone before he left?"

"No, sir."

"Didn't he give you a message for me?"

"No, sir."

The maid had moved off. Gérard stood there in the corridor, weak at the knees, feelings in turmoil. Lequesne had gone! Should he be glad or sorry? That very night he had decided to let the young man pursue the affair—and now his plans had been thwarted again! What exactly had happened in the garden last night? Had Luce discouraged Lequesne so emphatically that he preferred to leave? Had she turned down his advances? Had she pretended not to know what he meant? He must find her and question her, as soon as possible.

He hurried downstairs four steps at a time, and went into the dining room, where Luce was sitting at breakfast alone, eating a grapefruit in a glass dish.

IV

The questioning of Luce had not had the expected results. She reacted as if to an insult. She said she had made herself very pleasant to Lequesne, but their walk together was no more than friendly, her brother's assumptions wounded her deeply, and as for the sudden departure of her guest, she herself was more surprised than anyone, and would have some difficulty in getting her parents-in-law and her husband to excuse it. She certainly would not be seeing Lequesne again unless he was willing to apologize.

There was no more to be got out of her, painted, perfumed, silly creature that she was! And of course she might be telling the truth. Gérard decided to go and see Lequesne as soon as he returned to Paris. Lequesne was the only person who could give him precise information. Very likely he had been unable to bear the thought of staying under the same roof as Luce's husband. Come to think of it, such a misunderstanding would be an excellent excuse for a reconciliation . . . but he must act at once.

About four in the afternoon, Gérard pressed his friend's doorbell. He heard the bell ring, but nobody opened the door. He rang again, he knocked, but in vain. Neither Lequesne nor his mother was at home. This was a setback Gérard had not foreseen. He sat down on the top step of the stairs and waited for a few minutes, but he was in such a state of excitement that he could not stay there motionless. It would be better to come back later. Meanwhile, there was no reason why he shouldn't call at the shop. Tellier had caught the coach, along with Lequesne. He might be able to explain why Lequesne had returned to Paris so unexpectedly. Gérard ran downstairs, hailed a taxi, leaned back in the passenger seat, eyes closed and hands flat on his chest, and tried to breathe calmly.

94

He had not set eyes on the shop for two years. It had been repainted, bottle-green. The windows displayed balls of knitting wool, slippers, underpants and knitwear. Cheap underwear was set out on two stalls, one either side of the door. A solitary salesgirl was at her post there, out of doors: cold, cross, and with her hands jammed in the pockets of her grey overall.

"I'd like to see Monsieur Tellier, please."

"He's out. Business, was it?"

He hesitated a moment before replying, "Yes, business."

"Well, sorry."

"I can wait."

"If you want to. You'll find a chair by the counter. I'd better warn you, he'll be out quite a while yet, though."

Gérard went up two stone steps and into the shop. Its smell of dress fabric, disinfectant and dust choked him. The place was dark, its walls lined with black drawers with brass handles and labels on them. The counter, which was very long, occupied a third of the whole area. Gérard lit a cigarette to overcome the smell.

So this was where Tellier spent his days! In this subterranean gloom, among these acrid and mouldy odours. After hauling these dusty cartons about, snapping coarsely at the salesgirls, buttering up the suppliers, having a drink in some bar or other, counting his takings and putting up the shutters, he would go home, tired and dazed, with dirty hands, and the proud Elisabeth would open the door to him, raise her mouth to his the moment he came in! What on earth could she have found in the man to attract her? Perhaps it was his cripple's humility, the adoration felt for her by a failure?

A policeman came in, looking for the cape he had left in the shop while he was on the beat. He touched his cap and went out, shoulders swinging. A rat scurried across the room.

In the ensuing silence, Gérard thought he could hear the sound of his own breathing. His limbs relaxed in weary torpor. He must do something. It struck him that he might ask the salesgirl some questions. She did not know who he was. She might be able to tell him something useful about Tellier's management of the shop. But he was no good at chatting to "common people". He went to the door. What could he say? More or less at random, he asked, "I thought there were two sales assistants here?"

"That's right."

"Is the other one ill, then?"

"No. She might as well be, though, since I'm landed with all the work!"

"Then what *is* she doing?"

"Getting herself out of a mess!"

"And doesn't Monsieur Tellier mind?"

He thought she was going to jump down his throat, but instead she said, "Mind? Huh! Men! They'll talk and talk, but it doesn't take much to stop 'em in their tracks!"

"He's scared of her, is he?"

Instead of replying, she removed a pin from her overall and began to clean her dirty, varnished nails with it.

"I suppose she knows a lot about him?" he added.

This was a blunder. "What's it got to do with you?" She was staring at him, hands on her hips, eyes narrowed suspiciously, nose in the air. A weasel's face.

"Oh, nothing," he said. "But what I'd like to ask you—"

"I'm here to serve the customers, see? Not to chat to them. If you want explanations, ask 'em themselves when they get back!"

"When *they* get back? You mean they're out together?"

She saw her own mistake, and gave him a nasty look. "No idea!" she said.

"Where are they?"

"No idea."

She rocked back and forth like a naughty schoolgirl sent to stand in the corner. Gérard shrugged his shoulders. He supposed it must be some sordid business trouble between manager and salesgirl: something to do with cooking the books or swindling social security. No point in pursuing such trifles. He'd do better to telephone the apartment building

96

where Lequesne lived. The *concierge* should be able to tell him if his friend was back yet.

There was no telephone in the shop, but he had seen a bar on the pavement opposite, at the corner of the road.

The salesgirl was pacing from one end of her stalls to the other, handbag jammed under her armpit like the top of a crutch.

"I'm just off for a few minutes," said Gérard.

"Who shall I say called?"

"You needn't mention I was here." He tossed a five-franc coin on the pile of underwear and hurried off.

He was just about to go into the bar when he started in surprise, and drew back against the wall. Through the window, he had seen the familiar figure of Tellier, sitting beside a woman.

A moment passed. Gérard stepped forward and looked at them again. Neither Tellier nor his companion could see him; they were turned away from him, and deep in animated conversation. Suddenly, the unknown woman put her hand on the nape of Tellier's neck and brought her face close to his; in profile, it looked young and thin, with a large and painted eye like a hole in it. She was bare-headed, and wore the same grey overall as the other salesgirl. Tellier had not moved. The smoke from his cigarette rose above his head. That sly little paw with its scarlet nails was clinging to his thick neck.

His breath coming short, his legs quite weak with emotion, Gérard withdrew into the shelter of a shop doorway. He must have air! He was choking with hatred and elation. Now he knew all he needed! He must question the other salesgirl, make her talk, corner her and get her to tell all . . . With sudden frantic energy, he tore himself away from the support of the wall, took one step, two steps, and then began hurrying back to the shop.

The salesgirl received him with a grin. "Want some change, do you?"

He did not reply. Then he saw the girl's expression change to one of alarm, and she shrank back against the window.

97

Yes, he must look like a madman! His face had broken out in a sweat, and he was gasping and coughing, with his hands clasped at stomach level.

"What's the matter?" she asked. "What do you want?"

"Come inside the shop!" he panted. "I must talk to you."

He hardly recognized his own voice, so strangled did it sound. He felt a sudden surge of anger, directed at the poor girl, yet at the same time he could happily have collapsed on the ground and gone quietly to sleep in a corner.

"Listen, I haven't got time to beat about the bush," he said. "You know Mme Fonsèque?"

"Lady who owns the place? Yes."

"Well, I'm her son. Now, I've just seen Tellier and the salesgirl in that bar. I can guess it all, but I need the details, and if you won't talk I'll have you sacked. Sacked, understand?"

She shook her head, her face green as unripe fruit, stammering, "I—I don't know anything!"

"You're lying!" he shouted. "You told me too much, a little while ago, to be able to claim you don't know what's going on now!"

He grabbed her wrist and held it tight, but then, seeing her frightened expression, thought better of this approach and went on in a gentler tone. "You needn't pretend to me—in fact you have everything to gain by being frank! On the other hand, you'll be sorry for it if you won't talk. I can easily find some reason . . . Your job depends on you. Well, I'm listening."

He was quite surprised at his own powers of invention. He had a vague feeling that it was not himself at all talking like this, that he would never have known how to talk like this, that he was dreaming the whole thing. A cold draught of air chilled the sweat at his temples. The girl still said nothing.

"They're sleeping together, aren't they?" he asked.

She jumped, stared at him foolishly, and then opened her mouth. "No."

He stooped slightly, as if to come closer to her and transfix

98

her with his gaze. "They *were* sleeping together?"

"Yes."

Gérard felt his chest constrict violently. He was quivering with shameful satisfaction. He feared the girl might let him down, say something to spoil his pleasure.

"And now what?" he whispered.

"Now she's giving him what for!"

He laughed. "She doesn't want any more to do with him, eh?"

"*He* doesn't want any more to do with *her*!"

"Since when?"

"Since he got married. Well, a bit before he got married."

Disappointment welled unpleasantly up in him. But in his mind's eye, he could still see Tellier's heavy neck, and that clawlike hand digging into it, level with his hair.

"Then why is he meeting her in that bar?"

The salesgirl was getting a little self-confidence back. She pursed her lips. "Because she's got him where she wants him. She's telling him he's ruined her, she's got an inflammation of the womb, goodness knows what else, she needs to look after herself, her parents are giving her hell, she needs money . . . anything to make him cough up!"

By now he was letting her talk on, but he heard her no more than he heard the traffic noise in the street outside. It could not actually be said that Tellier had deceived Elisabeth, but this hole-and-corner affair was a good enough charge to bring against him! Elisabeth was sharing her bed with a back-of-the-shop Don Juan! Elisabeth was stepping into the shoes of a dirty and dishonest little tart! Elisabeth was begging for the caresses that had previously been lavished on this girl, with her grubby hair and her heavily made-up face. There was plenty here to humble her pride, plenty to give him a winning hand!

"What's her name?"

"Marcelle Audipiat."

"Where does she live?"

"40 rue Championnet."

He took out his notebook and wrote down the name and address, scribbling fast.

The salesgirl had opened her bag and was automatically powdering her face. When he had finished writing, she said,

"You won't say I told you, will you?"

"No. I promise."

"And I'll keep my job?"

"Yes, I promise that too."

She blew her nose. "Quite the young detective, eh?"

Looking at the girl, Gérard observed, with surprise and distaste, that she was recovering her composure, shaking herself, as it were, like a dog coming out of the water.

Tellier might be back at any moment. He must leave. But he was feeling too elated to go straight home, and by now he had ceased to take so much interest in the love affair of Lequesne and Luce. He remembered that Vigneral used to go to the Toc-Toc Bar every evening. Gérard had never set foot in the place, but he felt he ought to do something unusual, to bring a day which had produced so many useful surprises to a fitting conclusion.

*   *   *

The Toc-Toc Bar was bathed in an amber light, flattering to persons of more mature years. A negro was picking out notes on a piano in one corner with his big, dark hands. Tina, wearing a white jacket with blue revers, was agitating a cocktail shaker at ear level, pouring drinks in minute doses, chatting up customers, snapping at the waiter, taking money. It was seven o'clock, but all the bar stools were still occupied. Vigneral sat down at a table at the far end of the bar. Tina greeted him with a flutter of her fingers. The pianist smiled at him with carnivorous grace and put his foot down on the pedal, shaking his head. The waiter came over.

"A gin fizz, monsieur?"

"Yes, and a club sandwich."

He would eat lightly, wait for the place to close down, and

100

go to bed with Tina in a hotel room smelling of central heating pipes. The unvarying regularity of this programme was boring, but he needed the noisy, smoke-filled bar and the showy girl to get himself well and truly stupefied.

For today he had dropped the most appalling brick of his entire existence. And not for lack of warning himself against it, either! It had all happened with such diabolical ease. After finishing his day's work, he had gone to call on Gérard. Gérard was out, but Marie-Claude had been at home, and asked him into the drawing room. They stayed there almost an hour, talking in an easy, friendly way. Then—and what exactly had brought the subject up?—she had offered to show him a group photograph, taken last year, of her class at school. So they went into her room. He remembered the look of it: neat, demurely furnished, photographs of actors on the walls, smelling not of perfume but, faintly, of cold cream and powder.

He sat down on the arm of a chair, and she opened a drawer stuffed with pencils, erasers, postcards, odds and ends of fabric, and took out a typical school photograph stuck on a sepia cardboard mount. A gaggle of ugly little girls was ranged in two rows around a horse-faced woman.

"Can you find me in it?"

"No."

"I'm right at the top, beside the tall girl in glasses."

"What, that one? Dreadful little urchin looking like a delinquent unmarried mother? That's you?"

"Well, me a year ago! I don't think I've had that much time to change!"

She was laughing, leaning over his shoulder.

"What silly things we did that year! Mademoiselle Cuissard took us for maths, and one day a rag-and-bone man went down the road outside chanting his cry, and Mathilde Cohen started saying it was her father, and she had to talk to him. Mademoiselle Cuissard was simply furious! And there was another time when . . ."

She became quite voluble recalling her schooldays, with

101

vivacious, girlish gaiety. Vigneral had the odd feeling that he was an adult lost in a playground full of girls. He rather fancied the wolf-like character so suddenly thrust upon him. Marie-Claude was still talking away, breathing into his face with dangerous innocence. Then, suddenly, he felt sure her mind was not on what she was saying. Nor was his. They were both possessed by the same idea.

It was then, with the delightful sensation that he was doing something totally idiotic, that he had taken her hands, first one and then the other. She fell silent, rosy-faced, scared, teeth apart to show the pretty cavern of her mouth. He brought his own face closer to that waiting one, and still gazing into her beautiful eyes, larger than ever in anticipation of his kiss, so that they were a luminous, quivering, watery green, he had kissed her soft young skin: first he kissed her chin, then, gradually progressing, her cheek, and then her lips, which by now had come firmly and guilelessly together, feeding his hunger with nothing but the warm scent of make-up and her held breath. However, her whole body began to tremble in his arms, and when he started to draw away she bent her head and buried it in his shoulder with a birdlike movement.

At the time, to be sure, he had felt rather pleased with himself. Even when he left, half an hour afterwards, he was not dissatisfied with the episode. But now he was working out, in detail, all the unfortunate consequences of what he had done. He had trapped himself in a whole network of complications, and just for the fleeting pleasure of kissing a girl!

Suppose he took her to bed. No, mustn't think that way. Suppose he courted her decorously—touching rationed out, provocative little kisses, soulful glances? He could see no point in that. He had always thought of a young girl's love as a cheque that was likely to bounce. They got you all worked up, with an artlessness worthy of better employment, and then, when you wanted to let off steam, they backed out of it with outraged propriety. The only solution was not to see

102

Marie-Claude any more. That, however, would be a pity, since he liked her very much.

The real reason why all this had happened was that he had had about enough of Tina. She was a hysterical girl, only bearable in bed. He watched her bobbing about behind the bar like a puppet on a string. Later on she would come over to talk to him, tell him how she had been to see a fortune teller, or a girl friend had read the cards for her, or how she had dreamed of strange, naked women strutting on a dunghill—sheer nonsense!

At a nearby table, a woman he did not know—a woman of rather languid beauty, with the short-sighted eyes of a blonde and disenchanted lips—was sipping a geranium-coloured cocktail. She was obviously waiting for someone. It made Vigneral feel melancholy. His life, he thought, could be summed up as a constant succession of pretty woman, all of whom pleased him and some of whom detained him for a while—and he always regretted those he had not approached. He had the dismal impression of having spread himself out too thin. Too many envious glances at his neighbour's plate! Fonsèque used to tell him his eyes were bigger than his stomach, and Fonsèque was right. The thought of his friend brought him back to Marie-Claude again. He imagined her feeling confused, ashamed and elated after he left. He had promised to telephone her. Would he? No, he would not! No future in such childish games! Then, with a pang of remorse, he remembered her head nestling lightly on his chest, her small hands clinging to his jacket sleeve. He only had to kiss the girl and already, it seemed, he did not desire her any more, but he did feel a kind of brotherly, pitying tenderness.

Frowning, his eyes unfocused, he returned to lowering the level of the bubbles in his drink. He had taken only a few sips, however, when he nearly choked. Fonsèque had just entered the bar and was coming over to him. For a moment he thought his friend must have been "told all"—by whom?—and was about to make a scene. But Gérard simply sat down at his table and ordered "one of the same".

"Had dinner yet?" asked Vigneral.

"No."

"You haven't been home?"

"No."

This was a great relief. "What brings you here?"

"Oh, I felt like seeing you, that's all."

So everything seemed to be all right! Vigneral's awareness of having had a narrow escape made him feel well disposed to his friend, and it struck him that being with Gérard was a kind of contact with Marie-Claude. He'll be seeing her this evening, Vigneral thought, he may tell her what we talked about . . .

"I've been wanting to see you, too!" he said. "But it's ages since I've been able to catch you at home when I called."

Gérard laughed, pleased, rubbing his long, limp hands. "The fact is, I'm very busy at the moment."

"Work?"

"Yes."

"What—literary stuff?"

"In a way."

Good old Vigneral! If he only knew! If he only *could* know! For Gérard's secret weighed on him, making him feel almost ill. He shook his head, and mopped his face with his handkerchief. There were not enough people and not enough noise in this room. Today, a strange mood impelled him to wish for what he would normally dislike. The sandwich they had brought him was filled with disgusting Russian salad. The gin fizz tasted harsh as it went down his throat. The smoke stung his eyes.

"Marvellous—simply marvellous!" he said fervently, shuddering.

It must be nearly eight o'clock; groups of customers were leaving. When there were only a couple left, apparently glued to the bar, Tina removed her jacket and went over to the two young men.

"Do you know each other? Monsieur Fonsèque —

Mademoiselle Tina." Vigneral hated being obliged to introduce them. He was afraid of Gérard's critical disposition. What woman on earth could find favour with that impotent intellectual, his friend? Fonsèque would probably tell Marie-Claùde about his mistress, and he could imagine the kind of language he would employ! Wasn't that the best thing he could hope for, though, since he didn't want to see Marie-Claude again? All the same, he could not stand Tina's hanging around them. "Don't you have any customers to serve?" he asked.

"Why, no, honey-chile!"

Vigneral very much disliked being addressed as "honey-chile" in front of Fonsèque.

"I should think yours must be a very tiring job," said Fonsèque, with what Vigneral saw as highly suspect amiability.

"You bet your life it is, monsieur! I have to serve all kinds of people. Hey—I'm told you write! Didn't you say so, honey? That must be quite something!"

Vigneral winced, as if he had injured a nail. Evidently Tina wanted to dazzle Fonsèque with the freedom of her manners and her sparkling conversation. This was an utter disaster!

"Say, see that old boy sitting at the bar?" she went on. "He comes in here once a week, picks up some tart, takes her to a hotel, and gets her to hit him on the nose till it bleeds! Little taps with a ruler! Then he mops his nose up and sends her off with forty francs!"

"It sounds like a gift!" said Fonsèque.

"And then there's Monsieur Piédouche—he's the one who's written stuff about black magic. I bet you know all about black magic too, don't you?"

"Do leave him alone!" said Vigneral.

"Oh, you! You don't know the first thing about the occult! Honestly, monsieur, you never met anyone so materialistic! Seems a shame, with all his education and that!"

Fonsèque never took his eyes off the young woman: he was delighted to find she was so common and so stupid. It made him feel he was getting his own back on Vigneral and

105

everybody else. His friend went to bed with this girl! Other men had slept and would sleep with her. There would always be some man ready to waste his time pursuing and taking advantage of this wretched creature. The disproportion between the feelings she aroused and the value of the only recompense she was able to make was quite laughable. Love doesn't pay. He must remember that one. Meanwhile Tina, confident of her little triumph, was rolling her eyes in an oracular manner and pronouncing, sepulchrally, "And there are some things nobody can deny. Magnetism and telepathy and so on! You know Kekette who works shifts with me, honey? She organizes Black Masses, monsieur—she plays the part of Madame de Montespan in them! Would you like to go to one? I could fix it up!"

I'm sitting beside a depraved woman in a cocktail bar, thought Gérard, and my mother and sister have no idea where I am . . . It was all quite delightfully disgusting! He was carefully constructing a set of curious memories for himself.

He noticed the furious expression on Vigneral's face. No doubt he felt annoyed with Tina for making advances to his friend. How amusing it would be to make him, the professional ladykiller, jealous! He assured Tina politely, "What you say is most interesting. I think of Vingtras, Stanislas de Guafta, Eleonora Zagün . . . Satanism is a fascinating subject! There is a wonderfully realistic description of a Black Mass in Huysmans' *Là-bas*."

"Look, this time I really *can* see a customer trying to attract your attention!" snarled Vigneral.

Fonsèque and his friend stayed in the bar until it closed, and then they and Tina went to a nightclub nearby, which stayed open until three in the morning.

Gérard, having had two gin fizzes, was slightly drunk, but through his fuddled thought he knew he was in a state of great elation. Tomorrow, he thought, tomorrow . . . He smiled at the floor and the walls. Tina thought him extremely funny, "not at all like she'd expected". Although he said he couldn't dance, she dragged him out on the floor. He was often to remember that primitive, tom-tom rhythm, those distorted figures in the rainbow lights, their bodies coming together and drawing apart as if revolving round a hinge. Tina's face was tilted up to his, he could feel her breasts through her thin dress, and her legs moving like little animals. She was laughing. A gold tooth shone at one corner of her painted mouth. Passing Vigneral, she said, "Hi, honey!" and he turned his flushed and melancholy face towards them.

When the ragtime music stopped, Gérard thought he was going to throw up. He came back to the table. Sweat was running down into his eyes. Tina had collapsed against Vigneral and was sucking up the dregs in her glass through a straw. Fonsèque saw a purple scratch on her neck. He heard someone calling his name—"Gérard, Gérard!"—in a voice that seemed to come from out of doors and far away, and laid his head on his hot hands.

They had to take him home in a taxi.

V

Next day, Gérard did not come in until eight in the evening. As he was taking his coat off, he heard Luce's laughter, and remembered that Mme Fonsèque had asked her and her husband to dinner. He was late; the family had not waited for him before sitting down to eat. He opened the door, greeted the others, muttered a collective apology, and sat down in front of his plate of thick, lukewarm soup. He ate automatically, chin tucked in, eyes unfocused. His mind was entirely occupied by memories of the end of that afternoon. He could still see the proud, humiliated look on Elisabeth's face, could hear the level sound of her voice saying, "I knew." She countered everything he said with that calm affirmation. She had not asked him where he got his information. She had not tried to find out whether Tellier was still seeing his mistress (although Gérard had been purposely vague on this point). She had not been angry with him for poking his nose into her husband's private life. "I knew." But who had told her? Had Tellier confessed it all to her the day after their wedding? Had she found out by chance? And how could she bear to go on living with him if she knew? Could it be that he had a sensual hold over her? Did that base need govern her entirely? Did nothing matter to her but the overwhelming, if ungraceful, fact of physical possession? He couldn't bring himself to believe it! The scene had not been a long one; it had been in a sordid café where he took her when she came out of her office. In his mind's eye, he could still see the sawdust on the floor, the tables with their brass-rimmed marble tops, and Elisabeth in front of him, austere, unyielding and erect, as if she had an invisible wall behind her. Sadness and fury overcame him at the thought of such a wretched failure. His manoeuvres all thwarted, his hopes dashed—his conduct held up to ridicule, perhaps, in conversation between Elisabeth

108

and Tellier this evening! He was alone again. His weapons kept breaking in his hands, as they do in dreams.

He was so wrapped up in his troubles, that he let the conversation eddy around him, taking no notice of it. It was a pity his mother had asked the Aucocs to dinner. He would have liked as few faces and voices around him as possible today. One face and one voice had been quite enough—that sculptured face of hers, that steady voice saying, "I knew."

Gérard realized there was a different plate in front of him, and he was now eating meat and Russian salad. He remembered the Toc-Toc Bar, the club sandwich filled with fibrous leftovers, Tina wriggling about like a worm cut in half, Vigneral . . . he had been happy then! He had thought he was near his goal.

"Guess what time Gérard came in last night?" said Mme Fonsèque. "Three in the morning!"

She looked at her son with lugubrious pride.

Luce uttered a chuckle of clear laughter. "Goodness, have you taken to visiting nightclubs? Who's your boon companion, if I may ask?"

"Vigneral," said Mme Fonsèque. "Dear me, I never feel at ease when he's with that young man!"

Marie-Claude's knife clattered clumsily against her plate.

"Oh, don't say nasty things about our Vineleaf—he's a poppet!" said Luce. "I think he's looking very handsome these days. I'd mark him eighteen out of twenty!"

Marie-Claude did not look up. She was suddenly very busy cutting an already minute piece of bread in half.

"He's very much in the Van Gogh style, early period, don't you think, Marie-Claude?" said Paul casually.

"Er . . . I . . ."

"Don't you like the Nordic style?"

She blushed, and stammered, embarrassed but emphatic, "That depends whose it is!"

There was laughter, and then everyone started talking at once. Luce talked louder than the rest, grimacing, putting back her head to show off her firm, milky neck, the neck of a

109

redhead. Lequesne's defection did not seem to have upset her—unless she was playing a clever game to throw her husband off the scent. As if that plumply elegant fellow, so pretentious and foolish, was capable of suspecting anything!

Later, the conversation turned to cruises. Paul searched in his briefcase, which was always stuffed with photographs. He was looking for one of himself on the throne of Minos, but Luce insisted on showing them (instead) one in which he was seen offering a surprised Greek peasant a cigar. A negative was passed round, and had to be held up to the light.

"Oh yes, I can see perfectly," Mme Fonsèque was saying.

At last the family rose from the table and went into the drawing room for coffee. Gérard brought up the rear, looking bored, supercilious, and absent in spirit.

"Dear me, he looks like nothing on earth!" moaned Mme Fonsèque, and added, turning to him, "Oh, a letter came for you by the eight o'clock post, dear. It's in the hall if you want to get it."

He did, and walked away, glad of the excuse. The letter was lying on a salver with several leaflets from bookshops. He recognized Lequesne's handwriting and tore the envelope open, in the faint hope that this letter might at least offer him some consolation for his failure with Elisabeth. But his heart sank as he read the first few lines. Briefly, Lequesne informed him that he was leaving for London to take the tutorial post he had mentioned. "By the time you get this I'll be on my way to England." It was not an impulsive act, he said; he had thought it all out thoroughly in making his decision, and its great advantage was that it ended a situation as painful for him as everyone else. That was all. No word of coming back. The letter was written on the notepaper of the railway café where he had composed it. There was a postscript asking Gérard to make his apologies to Luce and the Aucocs.

Gérard folded the letter up again and put it in his pocket. He felt crushed by this latest shock. He was losing all round. Within a few hours, first Elisabeth and then Luce had escaped the traps he had set for them. He would have to begin all over again. No, he would have to give up the whole idea—he would never have the courage to embark upon such an unequal struggle once more. He had exhausted his strength and his resourcefulness. The blood rose to his face, humming in his ears, and a dull pain tugged at his eyes just behind the lids.

Why had Lequesne run away? Why was Elisabeth ready to accept the fact that Tellier had deceived her? Why did his own logical deductions always turn out wrong? Cowardice all round! Cowardice on his friend's part because he was afraid of failing and looking silly. Cowardice on Elisabeth's part because she could not do without a man who gave her pleasure at night. Both of them clinging to their small, fleeting satisfactions, fearing the dangers of freedom and adventure. You know what you are losing, but not what you might gain. And here was he, toiling away on behalf of these feeble creatures! Wearing himself out endeavouring to offer them a future of which they were unworthy! Was there no one who could live as he understood living? Was the entire world populated by those who clung timidly to familiar habits? Was the spirit of exploration, dignity and courage dead for ever?

On the other hand, perhaps Lequesne had too much respect for the institution of marriage to dare to attack it directly? A mistake: marriage in itself is not particularly worthy of respect, thought Gérard. A harmonious marriage, yes, because it is one form of human happiness. But if the marriage is grotesque, pathetic, merely physical, it ought to be destroyed in the very interests of the couple who had made a mistake in contracting it.

He heard voices and laughter in the next room. What would Luce say when she heard of her suitor's poor-spirited flight? She would probably be relieved. She wasn't worth any more than the others. Like the others, she would fear any interruption of her comfortable existence. Flirtation must not go beyond certain bounds . . . what a wonderful facility women have for giving themselves up body and soul to the first comer, while offering the next man thoughts of angelic

111

transparency! "Let there be courage in your love"—that was a fine remark of Zarathustra's! How could one arouse people as blind to passion as any bureaucrat, dotards of the heart, sleeping their way through marriage like so many dormice? Well, he ought to be thankful to them for giving him such good reasons to despise them!

Ideas were seething in his brain, so much so that he suddenly felt afraid of having a nervous attack. He had felt the same one evening when, coming home from a metaphysics lecture, he stood before his mirror asking himself in an undertone, "Who are you? Are you sure your name's Gérard Fonsèque? And the beings who live with you, whom you call mother and sisters—what are they to you, really?"

He was possessed by a similar delirium now, and a more dangerous one, because he knew its cause.

He saw before him the stuffed, one-eyed stag's head, coats hanging from its antlers. He took a curious pleasure in seeing them and himself as strange objects.

But to his surprise, he soon felt calmer. A glimmer of elation made its way through to the heart of his desperation. As if Lequesne's departure had really been a response to his most secret wishes! As if he had been hoping, all the time, that the trap would close on nothing! One man less between her and me, he thought, one man less! A pity about him, though.

He rose, went down the corridor, and opened the drawing room door.

"Now, you're not to have any more coffee, Paul!" Luce was saying. "You know how badly you sleep . . ."

"I'm tired," said Gérard. "I'm going to bed."

His mother fussed. Luce made jokes about the after-effects of a night on the tiles. Paul suggested bicarbonate of soda.

In his own room, he could still hear the sound of their conversation. "You know how badly you sleep . . ." He imagined Paul waking in the middle of the night, the sound of a voice thick with sleep, the movements of limp, satiated, clumsy bodies. Could one fight the alliance which creates the animal candour, between two beings, of sleeping together,

112

eating together, sharing the indignities of the flesh?

He thought, all at once, that his pretentions to saving Luce and Elisabeth from the dreary lives to which they had condemned themselves were ridiculous. He felt like those dogs that pursue a passer-by, yapping at his heels, jumping up and whirling round and wearing themselves out, while the object of their attentions goes on his way without even noticing.

Everything attempted outside oneself was useless, he thought. No man's isolation opens on to the isolation of his neighbours. Resignation to living for oneself alone, that was the thing!

The room had just been aired. Gérard got undressed quickly. It was a childhood habit of his to keep his socks on at night.

No sooner was he in bed than he felt sorry he had not stayed in the drawing room . . . What were they talking about now? Himself, perhaps? Or Lequesne? What was the listlessness he felt, constricting his throat, and making him suddenly want to weep? He put his head back, unconsciously seeking the regular breathing of slumber. Think of nothing any more. Dream of nothing any more. Sleep.

Later on, he did fall asleep, with his mouth open. He had forgotten to switch the light off, and it lit up his face till morning: a bloodless face like a wounded man's.

113

VI

Outside Gérard's room, Mme Fonsèque asked, "Am I disturbing you?"

"Yes." he said.

But she was already opening the door. She stood in the doorway, peering in at the unwholesome darkness of the room. Although it was day, the shutters were hardly open. Gérard was lying across his bed, one hand under his head, his dressing-gown open and showing his crumpled pyjamas. He was slowly smoking a cigarette. He had had breakfast in bed; she could see the tray with his empty cup and a saucer sticky with honey standing on a chair.

"Elisabeth's here. She wants to talk to you," she said.

He was up on his feet in an instant. "What?"

"She stayed away from the office on purpose to see you." Mme Fonsèque's voice was shaking oddly, and suddenly she moaned, "Oh dear, whatever has been going on between you two this time?"

He adjusted his garments, opened the window, and folded back the shutters with clumsy haste. "Nothing. Absolutely nothing, I assure you."

"Then why is she here?"

"How should I know?"

All the same, he turned his back to his mother, afraid that in the daylight from the street outside she might see the gleeful, gloating expression on his face. He added, as calmly as possible, "Go and get her, would you?"

However, she did not move, but stood there with her arms dangling, her face thrust forward, an imploring look on it. "Promise you'll be reasonable—please!" she faltered.

He flew into a brief temper. "Reasonable? What a thing to say! What are you afraid of, for God's sake? You love to dramatize the least little thing!"

114

"Don't you remember the last conversation you two had, before her wedding?"

He went red, and muttered that all that was old history now. Shaking her head, Mme Fonsèque went out.

Gérard leaned against the wall and closed his eyes, to help himself overcome the confusion of his mind. What did his sister want? He had had enough of fencing and craftiness! Whatever attacks might be made on him now, he would refrain from replying. He would not fight back. This resolve gave him a sense of relief that quite surprised him. It was as if the decision put him beyond anyone's reach; nothing could harm him now!

He did not move a muscle when Elisabeth came in. She had kept her mackintosh on, and wore a hat with a small brim which showed her face: it looked pale and ill. She was not wearing any lipstick, her eyelids were swollen, and her eyes shone with a clear and icy grey, like a steel blade.

She sat down on the chair her brother offered her, but without leaning back in it. She said nothing. He had no intention of breaking the silence himself, for fear of starting the conversation off on the wrong foot.

Suddenly she shook her head, and began to speak in a frantic, toneless voice that was painful to hear. "What you told me about Joseph wasn't really true, was it, Gérard? Not really?"

"Didn't you tell me you knew all about it?"

Elisabeth shivered, and turned huge eyes on him. "I was lying. I didn't know. But I was sure you must be wrong."

His heart seemed to have stopped. Astonishment stunned him. He felt nothing but the desire to remain upright, not to weaken or show any vulnerability in front of her.

"So now?" he said.

Elisabeth's face suddenly twisted. She was visibly struggling with her rebellious pride. "Yesterday evening, I told Joseph what you'd told me," she murmured. "Don't worry, I didn't drag your name into it. I invented an anonymous letter and said it had come in the morning and I'd torn it up at once. I

115

kept on asking him questions, I insisted on answers, I begged him to defend himself . . ."

"And?"

"He told me he did have a mistress before we were married, but he'd stopped seeing her."

He was filled with an ugly joy. His decision not to embark upon argument forgotten, he asked, in a humorous tone, "And did he tell you the lady's identity?"

"I didn't ask."

"Oh, you should have! The details are rather spicy. A salesgirl. One of the girls in our shop. A common little tart in an overall, with grubby hair—"

"What's that got to do with it?" she asked wearily.

He was indignant. "How do you mean, what's that got to do with it? Don't you mind being neglected for a vulgar girl who sees to it that she gets paid for going to bed?"

"The question is whether I really am being neglected. He swore he'd broken it off with her the day after I said I'd like to be seeing him again, but I've no proof of it. Can I believe him? *Ought* I to believe him? You're the only person who can tell me."

Gérard had never seen a woman looking so shattered. It had taken this unsavoury business over Tellier for her to lose control over herself entirely, show herself to him in disarray, weak and anxious, licking her wounds, begging for reassurance with her eyes.

The pitiful change in her both disgusted and delighted Gérard. He was recovering his dominance over events just when he thought they had got the better of him. The whole future of the Telliers depended upon him alone. One word, one sentence and other people's lives would take the course he chose for them. The responsibility of it aroused sensations of lively alarm.

"Daren't you tell me?" breathed Elisabeth.

He turned his head away. What should he say? He felt tempted to tell her Tellier had not deceived her after all. But that would mean casting her back into the dreary existence

116

which he wanted her to escape. Weren't there occasions when bearing false witness was elevated to the level of a positive duty? He must lie, in Elisabeth's own interests . . . no, why pretend to himself? There was one thing certain: he couldn't let a chance like this slip through his fingers! Against such an adversary, any weapon was legitimate!

"You don't say anything. You're being tactful. You don't know how much your tactfulness hurts!" she went on.

He went over to his sister and put a hand on her shoulder with a rapid, shamefaced gesture. She looked up at him, raising a thin face with eyes as docile as a dog's in it. He guessed she was devoured with impatience, and delayed the blow out of mingled pity and cruelty, relishing his own calm in contrast to her distress. He noticed the vein on her forehead standing out as it had on the evening of their last argument. Her mouth was trembling, and she held her hands so tightly pressed together that her knuckles seemed to be edged with paler skin. He began speaking, gently.

"I wish I could set your mind at rest, Elisabeth, or at least say nothing. I'm afraid you'll hold it against me if I speak out."

She kept her eyes fixed on his lips. "No, I won't!" she whispered. "Hurry up!" She sounded like a sick woman at the end of her tether, begging the doctor to get it over with quickly.

"But will you believe me?"

"Why should you want to lie?"

He felt as if he were jumping into the void, eyes wide open and heart empty of all emotion, as he said softly, "Well, you did ask for it, then . . . yes, he's deceiving you, Elisabeth. He's deceiving you with that girl."

He stopped, surprised by his own spite and audacity. Self-disgust rose up in him, along with fear. It briefly occurred to him to contradict what he had just said—but no, it was too late. This was just a bad moment to be endured. Later on he would enjoy his hard-won triumph. He leaned over his victim to see what he had done to her. Her mask-like face was rigid

117

with a kind of humiliated amazement. She said, in a voice he could hardly catch, "Are you sure?"

"Do you think I could bring myself to tell you if I weren't?"

"How did you find out?"

"I saw them both sitting in a bar, making eyes, kissing, caressing each other—"

"It isn't true!" she cried out.

"I told you you wouldn't believe me."

"Oh, I'm sorry—I don't know what I'm saying."

Feeling horribly as though he were cutting into living flesh, he went on. "So I went straight to the shop and talked to the other salesgirl. She told me all about it."

"I don't want to know any more."

"But you will know more—you must, Elisabeth! Yes, he knew this girl before your marriage, but he hasn't broken with her at all. He's still seeing her. He's giving her money. He has to give her money, to get her to go to bed with him. At the moment she's ill, and it's all his doing. He may even have made her pregnant."

She was shaking her head, as if to deny this final insult.

"Elisabeth, I don't suppose you expected anything like this, but for some time I've been suspecting that he led a double life. I must admit, though, I was staggered by what I found out. I wish I could feel there was any doubt about it, but I've seen them—I've seen them!"

He was consumed with fury now, relentless in pursuit of the exhausted woman, and the wounds he inflicted on her struck deep into himself. He felt both wretched and triumphant. He couldn't stop now! He feared the sudden silence which had fallen between them again. "Look, I've got names, and dates . . . "

He took his notebook out of his pocket, but Elisabeth raised a hand to stop him.

"No, I think you really *should* know. Her name is Marcelle Audipiat, and she lives at 40 rue Championnet. We'll go and see her together if you like, question her. You can meet your successful rival, hear news of your defeat from her own

118

lips—in return for a sizeable tip! Right, let's go. We'll take a taxi."

He was insistent, feeling quite sure that she would refuse to go with him.

"Come on!" he repeated. "Then at least you'll know I'm telling the truth. You'll have bought yourself certainty."

"I'm certain enough already," she sighed.

He fell momentarily silent, breathing hard, exhausted and elated. Then he sat down beside her and took her icy hands between his own.

"You're unhappy, and I feel responsible," he said. "But I know you'll thank me later. The man didn't love you, never loved you. He started his affair up again almost as soon as he was married; that shows you what he's like—and he chose a woman of his own kind. Elisabeth, darling, I wish I could comfort you and tell you it isn't true, tell you to go back to him, live with him again . . . but I simply can't! What are you planning to do now?"

She was looking straight at the wall in front of her, silent and tense. He wished she would burst into healing floods of tears—tears that would fling her into his arms, gasping, limp and defeated. "What are you planning to do?" he repeated.

"I don't know," she said.

"Do you feel you could ever forgive him?"

"No."

He heaved a sigh of relief. "Would you contemplate a divorce?"

"I'm not contemplating anything. I want to be left alone."

She stood up. She was so pale that he thought she was going to faint. He felt worn out himself, quite ill with anxiety, self-disgust, and a sudden compunction. As if in a dream, he saw her move away, her mackintosh rustling with a rubbery sound.

She reached the door, and then he caught up with her and took her by the elbow. "Listen, you can't go home for lunch. Stay here till you feel better—stay and think things over."

She put the palm of her hand to her face. She was holding a

119

handkerchief crumpled up into a ball like a white pebble, and her nostrils looked pinched. Suddenly she closed her eyes and bowed her head.

"Why?" she moaned. "Why, oh, why?"

VII

The disused bedroom was re-opened, Elisabeth's bed brought up from the basement, the big wardrobe cleared of the summer clothes that had been stored in it since her marriage. Elisabeth's beige dressing-gown, her tooth-glass, her powder box and her set of brushes reappeared in the bathroom. Lunchtime became half past twelve, to fit in with her office hours.

Mme Fonsèque fluttered round her daughter as if she were a convalescent, sighing a great deal and showering questions on her. "I just can't make out why you've left him!"

"We had a quarrel," said Elisabeth.

"Well, make it up, then! If people separated every time they had a little quarrel no marriage would ever last! Do you want me to do it for you?"

"No."

"How long are you staying here?"

"Until I've come to a decision."

"But at least you're not planning to divorce him, are you?"

"I don't know."

Tellier came to the Fonsèques' apartment on several occasions, hoping to see his wife. Every time Elisabeth refused to leave her room, and Mme Fonsèque talked to her son-in-law in the drawing room. When she saw him looking so devastated, his eyes red and his voice hoarse, she could not help sympathizing with him. The poor man begged her to help him and assured her that he was not to blame.

"Then what *have* you done to her?" exclaimed the good lady.

"That's for her to tell you, since she doesn't believe me."

He asked her to give Elisabeth interminable letters and make sure she read them. Then he would leave, looking wretched, and asking for permission to come back; he would thank her over-effusively, blow his nose, and reluctantly make for the door.

Mme Fonsèque would emerge from these interviews both tearful and furious, to go straight to her daughter.

"Whatever he's done, I'm sure he's not a bad man. Look, here's a letter he gave me for you."

Elisabeth tore up his letters without even looking at them. After a while she told her mother not to carry messages for Tellier, but the good lady dared not tell her son-in-law about this, and decided to keep the unopened envelopes in a box. Reluctantly, she explained to her friends that Elisabeth had come home while her husband was busy travelling about. Luce and Paul were told not to ask Elisabeth any questions and avoid all allusions to this stupid quarrel. The young couple's visits became less frequent.

Mme Fonsèque herself soon stopped asking her daughter questions. She was able to watch her at close quarters, and saw how thin, pale and remote she was. She realized that her own love could do nothing to help her child, rigid as she was with wounded pride. Her inability to help Elisabeth made her feel ill. She slept poorly, waking with a stiff neck and a buzzing in her ears; she lost her appetite and could not stand the sight or smell of a plate of meat. One evening she felt as if she were suffocating. She fainted away beside her bed; no one knew anything about it. She came back to her senses to find herself lying fully clothed on the bedside rug. Her head was ringing as if she had had a blow on it, and she was shivering. She was frightened and thought of calling a doctor, but she felt better next day.

When Gérard was alone with her he took her to task for her lugubrious attitude. "Anyone would think you didn't like having your daughter here!"

He himself was exultant, and active in his elation. He had already consulted a lawyer in secret, about grounds for divorce and "the price to be paid".

However, he dared not broach this subject to Elisabeth yet. First and foremost he had to cure her, purge her of her feminine past. He therefore confined himself to surrounding

122

her with cumbersome solicitude. He took her to the office, and came to meet her at the end of the day, so that Tellier would not be tempted to approach her in the street. He bought her flowers. He offered to take her to the theatre or the cinema. Generally she refused these invitations, but once he took the whole family to see a film which had been highly praised in the Press. It turned out to be a silly, sentimental story, full of moist kisses, partings under gas lamps, babies' cradles foaming with lace like so many cream buns. When the lights went on again he thought he saw Elisabeth dabbing surreptitiously at her eyes. He did not press her to go out to a show again. He himself preferred evenings spent at home, where he could feast on her presence as if it were actual nourishment. For hours on end she was his, she fed his devouring hunger. Occasionally he felt he could not keep her within reach of his vision without her husband's face surfacing in the background, looking like some grotesque fish. But sometimes he felt as if she had never left home, and was still the same intelligent and austere young woman whose secret heart he could never discover. She would rise to her feet, sit down again, pick up or put down her knitting, and his swift, greedy, miser's eyes caught her slightest gesture in passing. Oh no, he was not sorry for the questions he had asked, the efforts he had made, the lies he had told! He would have done it all over again, every day, to keep her here in her proper place, at the mercy of his love.

"I am ridiculously happy," he wrote in his diary, and indeed, he felt so much at ease in this equivocal situation that his colour improved and he put on a little weight.

He had forgotten his failure over Lequesne. He cracked jokes with Marie-Claude, to keep himself in form. One evening he even read extracts from his essay on Evil aloud to his united family, and was delighted to realize that nobody understood a word of it.

*   *   *

123

Marie-Claude could not sleep. Sitting up in bed, craning her neck, her eyes open in the familiar darkness of her room, she was thinking about her happiness. She had not seen Vigneral since the day he kissed her—three weeks of humiliating anxiety had passed without any sign of life from him—and now, this very evening, he had come to meet her when she came out of her lecture. He had apologized, pleading a cold and pressure of work. He seemed to be on edge, ill at ease and guilty, and begged her to believe him. And so she did, simply because he was there again.

It was half past five, and dark, and he took her for a walk in the deserted Tuileries. The gardens were misty, and the air smelled of damp gravel. Inky pools quivered at the statues' feet. They had sat down on a wet, freezing bench, and he suddenly took her in his arms. His breath rose from his lips in pale vapour, and little drops of water glistened on his fair hair.

Once again she remembered the weight of his cold face against hers, the thirsty touch of his mouth on hers, forcing it open, penetrating it, searching it with his tongue, then wandering, breathless and tender, along her cheek, into the hollow of her neck and down to her bare, numb hands. Passers-by turned to look at them, but Vigneral did not let go of her. He kept saying the most peculiar things: "Marie-Claude, my little Marie-Claude, you've got to believe me, I'm no worse than most! I expect Gérard said we went out together, I expect he mentioned a girl to you . . ."

"No—no, he didn't."

She did not see what he was getting at. She let his voice lull her; it was hoarse with emotion and male tenderness. Suddenly it seemed a very simple, natural thing to be snuggling into a young man's shoulder, in public gardens where anyone might see them. When he moved, she could hear his wallet rustling in the inside pocket of his jacket. She felt there was a drip on the end of her nose, but she didn't mind. He bent over her again, and this time she had her mouth open ready for his kiss.

Now, sitting in the pitch dark, a feverish excitement kept her awake. She was trembling all over. Her hands were damp and her parted legs were sticking to the sheets. She thought she could still savour the scent of his breath and the frosty air on her bruised lips.

"Oh, I love him, I'm so proud, I'm so happy!" she kept telling herself in an undertone.

She was, indeed, brimming over with happiness. It was too bad she couldn't tell anyone. She switched the light on, took a locked notebook out of her bedside table drawer, and drew a mysterious little circle bristling with rays on that day's page. She would remember the secret significance of that drawing for the rest of her life.

She got out of bed and began pacing up and down the room in her nightdress, looking at herself in the worn wardrobe mirror as she passed it. Suddenly she thought she looked beautiful, and wished Vigneral were there to admire her. What was he doing now? Was he asleep? Was he thinking of their meeting? She wouldn't be seeing him again for two days. She sighed, adjusting a slipping shoulder strap, and plunged her warm little hand into her hair. Tomorrow she would pin up that picture of Fred Colmar, the actor, over her bed; he looked rather like Vigneral. Then he would watch over her sleep and no one else would guess a thing! It was a deliciously exciting idea.

Oh, how hot it was in here! She turned the radiator right off, fanned herself briefly with an exercise book, and then decided to go to the kitchen for a glass of water.

Out in the corridor, she saw that Elisabeth's door was ajar. Perhaps her sister couldn't sleep either? She longed to be able to talk to someone before she went back to bed. She pushed the door open. It was dark in the bedroom, and her sister's regular breathing scarcely broke the silence. She asked, in a low voice, "Are you asleep, Elisabeth?"

"No—what do you want?"

She shivered with pleasure. "Oh, nothing! I was only going to the kitchen to get a glass of water. Can I come in?"

125

"Hadn't you better go back to bed?"

"I'm not sleepy."

She went into the room, firmly switching the light on. But when she saw Elisabeth's calm face she could not think just what to say. To cover the awkward moment, she stretched and rubbed her eyes. She really wanted to talk about Vigneral, speak his name, evoke his memory. She was looking for a way of bringing him into the conversation without any risk of betraying their secret. Coming to a sudden, bold decision she asked—her eyes furtive, her heart beating fast—"Do you know who I met today?"

"No."

"Vigneral! Elisabeth, what do you think of him?"

"Did you get up at midnight to ask me what I think of Vigneral?"

The blood rose to Marie-Claude's face. "Well, no!" she faltered. "I only mentioned him because I happened to see him. So what *do* you think of him?"

Elisabeth shrugged her shoulders. "A nice young man—not very bright, rather a roving eye."

"I don't agree with you at all!" cried Marie Claude. She was up in arms, and was already feeling sorry she had broached the subject with someone who could never understand! She continued heatedly. "Vigneral has not got a roving eye! He just pays attention to women, and people notice!"

"They notice, yes. That's what I mean."

"And he's not stupid either! He's not clever in the same way as Gérard, that's all! You see everything through Gérard's eyes these days!"

"Oh, my poor child!" Elisabeth was looking at her sadly.

There was a moment's silence, and Marie-Claude seized her chance to make for the door. She did not want her pleasure spoiled any more! How blind and thoughtless people were! Telling anyone about her happiness meant losing part of it directly. She was going out of the room when Elisabeth called her back.

"You didn't tell me where you met him?"

She turned, in anger and pride. "He came to meet me out of my lecture!"

She waited for her sister to utter exclamations, ask questions, show flattering surprise. She felt the curious sensation of having dropped a brick which *had* to be dropped.

"Is he quite crazy?" inquired Elisabeth in a calm tone which exasperated Marie-Claude.

"I don't know what you mean!"

"Well, what did he want?"

"You may well ask!"

"I suppose he said something to explain what he was doing there?"

"Yes."

"Well, what was it?" Elisabeth asked again.

"Suppose we say that's a secret between him and me!" Marie-Claude was smiling loftily, and preening herself, as she stood there in her nightdress.

"Marie-Claude come over here. Let me hold your hands. He wasn't making up to you, was he?"

"Yes, he was!"

"Did he tell you he loved you?"

"Yes."

"And you believed him?"

"Yes."

"Oh, darling, this is ridiculous! He was making fun of you!"

"What do you know about it?"

"Listen, he has a mistress. He'll make up to any woman if he thinks there's a chance of getting her into bed, but young girls like you don't interest him at all. At least, I hope they don't!"

"That's not true!" cried Marie-Claude. "It's not true!" She had gone very pale, and her eyes were flashing furiously in her childlike face.

"You mustn't see him again," Elisabeth went on. "Promise me you'll tell him—"

"I won't promise you anything! I won't tell him anything!

127

I'll see him any time I like! He loves me and I love him, and you don't know anything about it, you only want to hurt me, and I never ought to have told you—oh, I was so happy before I did!"

Her chin began to tremble and the corners of her mouth drooped, but she was not crying. "Move up, will you?" she muttered, and sat down on the edge of the bed beside her sister. Elisabeth put a bare arm round her shoulders.

"He's so kind and strong and handsome! You don't know him! If you did you'd love him too . . ."

"There, there!" said Elisabeth. "I didn't mean to hurt you, dear. Calm down . . ." She felt the frail little body breathing unevenly against her shoulder. All she could see of Marie-Claude's bowed head was her light chestnut hair. A desperate, hot little paw grabbed her own hand under the bedclothes.

"We went to the Tuileries, this afternoon . . . we sat on a park bench . . ." Suddenly she stopped. "Would you turn the light out, Elisabeth?"

"Why?"

"I don't know . . . we'd be more comfortable."

Elisabeth pressed the switch, and Marie-Claude's urgent voice went on with its story in the dark.

But while Marie-Claude talked, an infinite sadness swept over Elisabeth, carrying her away from her sister. The exuberance of Marie-Claude's passion abashed her: it violated her new-found isolation. She had been through it all: the same excitement, and pride, and obsessive tenderness. She had lost it all! It was like having her own past happiness flung in her face! How useless and paltry she suddenly felt before this glowing girl!

Marie-Claude stopped. Only then did Elisabeth realize she had not actually been listening. She ought to scold her, and perhaps give her some good advice. She could not bring herself to do it. Leaning her head back, she looked at the pale patch which was Marie-Claude's face in the dark, her eyes shining in it like water at night. She touched the girl's smooth cheeks and neck and childish lips. Abruptly, a spasm shook

128

her. She was too unhappy! She couldn't bear it any longer. She was going to cry out. Heaving sobs rose into her mouth. "Go back to bed," she whispered. "Go to sleep, Marie-Claude, dear."

"Am I bothering you?"

"No, no."

"Not cross, are you?"

"Just a bit tired . . . leave me alone now, would you?"

"You won't tell Gérard or Mother?"

"What? No, no, I won't! Now, off you go . . ."

Marie-Claude dropped a quick kiss on her forehead. Elisabeth heard the sound of a pair of bare feet on the floor.

Left alone, she buried her face in the pillow and waited grimly for the tears to come.

Next day, Elisabeth left the Fonsèques' apartment and went back to her husband. Two weeks later they left for Metz, where Joseph Tellier had accepted a job with good prospects in a branch of the Aucocs' business. This unexpected flight upset Gérard badly. His mother tried her best to get him to take some interest in the shop, but he refused point blank. So Mme Fonsèque sold it.

PART THREE

I

After several months' respite, Mme Fonsèque fell ill again.
She would suddenly drop off to sleep in the middle of the day,
while cramp kept her awake at night. She would sit up in bed
rubbing her calves under the bedclothes and trying not to cry
out. Sometimes the ends of her fingers swelled up, and when
she put a hand to her cheek it felt oddly cold and unyielding,
like dead meat. She grew thinner. Her vision was blurred. One
morning, Gérard came into her room after breakfast and
found her huddled in her armchair, her dress unbuttoned, her
hair undone, with a basin on her knees. She was vomiting
blood. She looked at him, raising a pale face with swollen,
slobbering lips and large, melting, uncomprehending eyes.
She was panting quietly, and tried to smile. A doctor was
summoned at once. He looked at her grey, shrivelled tongue,
took a blood sample, said something about uraemia,
prescribed serum and glucose injections, and bled her; this
gave her a little relief. But Gérard guessed the end was near.
He went through the next few weeks like a somnambulist.

The family home became an encampment. Luce sometimes
came to spend the night, and would fuss about from early in
the morning, wearing a white smock with a monogram on it,
painted and perfumed, distresed and perfectly useless. Paul
Aucoc paid formal calls, his gloves in his hand, his detachable
collar funereal in appearance, his voice pitched low. Marie-
Claude would shut herself up in her room for a good cry. As
for Elisabeth, Mme Fonsèque did not want her eldest
daughter to be bothered "for a little illness which may not be
anything much". She took her scruples to the lengths of
having the daily bulletins on her health which were sent to
Metz read aloud to her first.

However, her illness was beyond the treatment the doctor
prescribed for it. They sometimes thought she had stopped

133

breathing, but a few seconds later her chest would begin rising and falling again with increasing strength, going faster and faster. She would take great gulps of air, and then her breathing would fade away again until it was barely perceptible. Ulcers appeared on her gums. Her temperature dropped below normal and her pulse slowed.

The Telliers, informed by telegram, arrived a few hours before she died. To his amazement, Gérard saw that Elisabeth was wearing loose dresses to conceal her swollen belly. She was seven months pregnant. The mere thought of it would have filled him with disgust in other circumstances; in his present state of distress, however, it seemed that nothing more could affect him.

Mme Fonsèque died in a coma. Joseph Téllier was the one who took charge of the necessary arrangements. He discussed the type of funeral, the grant of a site for the grave, the printing of cards: acting with authority, disposing with authority of matters which were nothing to do with him. Gérard, however, had no spirit left to intervene. He did not want to do anything that would distract him from his grief. He was like a small child in a mourning household, unable to understand or support anyone. Nobody asked his opinion; they scarcely even troubled to tell him what decisions had been taken.

He went to Mme Fonsèque's room in secret after she had been put in her coffin, and looked at it; tidy, cold, prepared for emptiness. An unpleasant memory came back to him: "There are always bloodstains in the room where a dead person spent his last night!" He fled into the corridor and closed his eyes, as he had long ago, to shut out the picture of the brown leather sofa crouching against the wall like a satiated beast, a picture hanging crooked above it.

They draped the front door with black, the hall was filled with mountains of flowers, and the apartment was full of that pressed-flower scent which reminded Gérard of his sisters' weddings. The candles had a powerful smell, too, and the silver candlesticks shone with chilly brilliance in the shadows.

After an interminable funeral service, the body was taken to the cemetery by hearse. It was a day of gusty showers. Puddles of yellow water were slowly forming in the grave. Shivering, Gérard saw his three sisters huddled round that muddy hole like crows around their nest. Under their mourning veils they were dabbing at their eyes with white handkerchiefs. Elisabeth's belly strained the black fabric of her dress. That grotesque swelling, with new life forming within it, was at sinister odds with the gaping trench at their feet. Gérard could not take his eyes off it; a heaving mound, a disgustingly full pouch, an abhorrent burden which deformed Elisabeth, swelling her to the rounded shape of a spoon. They ought not to have let her come.

The coffin was slowly lowered, rain running down its sides and on to its brass handles. There was a gust of wind, and the three sisters grabbed at their black skirts as they blew up, showing their pale pink underclothes. A sob arose from them. They were crying as they clutched their billowing skirts against their thighs with that wanton gesture.

Now the big, varnished coffin was at the bottom of the hole, and the ropes still linking it to human hands let it go. In between the walls of earth, the wooden box lay exposed to the rain. The first spadefuls of soil fell sonorously on its lid, as if it were a drum. The undertaker supervised the work: he was freshly shaven, sombre, and fat as a carrion crow. In a few seconds it would all be over. Gérard remembered his mother's affectionate, sensitive, worried eyes. Now they were throwing clods of clay at her face, she was opening her mouth to protest, the clods were filling it, and ropes slid past her slack limbs. He leaned over the hole, at the risk of toppling over. His head was whirling. He wanted to cry out, call, struggle. A firm arm moved him away, supporting his shoulders. The undertaker smelled of peppermint.

Gérard realized he was being led away and made to sit down on a bench. Ranks of old grey tombstones stood in front of him, bristling with iron crosses, sullied with miserable bunches of flowers. He was shivering. His throat hurt. He noticed several glass beads mingling with the wet gravel at his feet. The whistle of a train broke the silence. How lonely he was now! He recalled past joys: his mother's words and movements and phrases. Suddenly an icy future loomed before him, like his own grave, a future in which he would have to live without her. He thought of the deserted rooms, the deep silence, the isolation of his future existence . . .

Enormous clouds rolled over the sky; they looked as if they were munching éclairs. Footsteps approached. Tellier was walking at the head of the party, an expression on his face as of a man who has seen a job well done. He was wiping his forehead with a handkerchief the size of a towel. Elisabeth was waddling along behind him like an overfed chicken. Her veil was put back, showing a face exhausted by grief and pregnancy. Luce followed, leaning on her husband's arm and sniffling quietly, he was patting her hand and looking grave. He'd be consoling her tonight. Then came Marie-Claude, Vigneral, the elder Aucocs, family friends, all tramping along as if to a soup kitchen. They stopped when they came to him. Was he feeling better? Would he like something to drink?

Taxis were loaded up, taking the family home. In the taxi, Tellier cleaned the mud off his shoes with a piece of wood. Luce took of her hat, which was squeezing her temples.

They had to stop at a charcuterie on the way to buy something to eat.

II

The silence of the apartment oppressed Gérard so much that he did not like to move his head on the pillow. It was not an absence of noise: it was the quiet breathing of a void, as if the floors and walls of the building had disappeared from around his room and he were left alone, perched in a vacuum, as if at the top of a chimney. And then the faint sound of crockery, of a child's voice, gradually reconstructed the building for him room by room. But it was all so far away, so high above, so deep below, that there was still silence around him. It seemed to him that he would always be carrying this dense, vast, indifferent silence with him, like some marginal area impervious to human contact.

He closed his eyes, and the red darkness behind his eyelids rather alarmed him. His temperature had gone down all right, but the pain in his joints would not allow him to get up. He had caught cold at the funeral; the day after it, a savage pain had stiffened the joints of his knees and elbows. Taking the dispensing chemist's advice, Marie-Claude had bought him some colchicine tablets for gout, but the doctor, who was called in shortly afterwards, diagnosed rheumatic fever. The treatment he prescribed included bed rest and a strict diet; and a bottle of salicylate tablets replaced the colchicine, which Gérard had only just begun to take, on his bedside table. He swallowed one tablet an hour, with considerable distaste. He perspired whenever he moved, his ears felt blocked and deaf, and the mere thought of making any effort was wearisome.

The Telliers had been to see him before they left to return to Metz. Joseph displayed an infuriating sympathy for his brother-in-law. Obviously, Elisabeth had not told him that Gérard was to blame for the breach between them. She had gone back to the man without any explanation, returning to his den because she was pregnant. Now, reunited with her husband, she was resuming the dreary way of life she had so nearly escaped. Nothing could affect her now. Even their mother's death did not hurt her as much as it hurt her brother. She had a shameful remedy for her grief within hand's reach, within mouth's reach. So did Luce. And maybe Marie-Claude too. Or at least, Marie-Claude was hoping her future might hold some wonderful encounter. But he had nothing, never would have anything to distract him from his sorrow. The one person who would not have left him for someone else had just died.

Sometimes he felt choked by affection as the memories of his mother flooded back to him. At other times, he thought he felt nothing any more, and was alarmed by that terrible vacuum. Then he would think of the varnished oak coffin slipping down between those walls of clay, down and away from him, disappearing from sight, spattered with earth and rain, and a spasm of love and horror would take him by the throat again.

Silence and solitude made him afraid. Where on earth was Marie-Claude? It was six o'clock, and her lecture finished at four on Wednesdays. Yesterday, at the cost of great pain, he had dragged himself to his sister's room so as to copy out the timetable pinned to the wall. Now he could follow her all through her days . . . but what does a timetable really tell about anyone? The true essence of Marie-Claude still escaped him through the network of numbers. He knew no more about her than she would let anyone know. Was she in love? Maybe not. But a day would come when he must envisage that disaster. *She* would go through it, just like the others. This time, however, the stakes were too high for him to let her go. He would keep her whatever his reasons for doing so must be. Once, he had believed he was working for his sisters' own good. The time for such sentimental pretence was over now. It was his own happiness he was fighting for, just as he would have fought to save his skin. He needed them! He couldn't live without them. This apartment had once been a place full of high voices, pretty dresses, long hair—was it to become an

138

empty shell with life withdrawing from it like the tide? His childhood had been spent among those feminine faces and soft hands; was it going to end in isolation and tedium? Oh, the voluptuous satisfaction of knowing that no one else's influence conflicts with yours in the heart of a dear one, no image matters more than yours, that you literally possess that heart! Marie-Claude often used to say, "Oh, I thought of what you were saying last night . . .", or, "Today's lecture would have amused you . . ." Such scrappy comments at least showed that she thought of him when she was away from him, that she saw everything in relation to him, she lived for him! What more could he wish for? It was pleasant, when she came into his room, to see her touch the clothes lying on his chair, his books, his papers. Then her casual gesture took on a connotation of infinite tenderness which made him feel wonderfully happy. He loved Marie-Claude more than ever now that she was the only one of his sisters he had left. His attention had once been shared between the three of them; now it was all hers, concentrated on her alone. He was not interested in the others any more! Luce had taken Lequesne's departure with scarcely feigned indifference. The cowardly Elisabeth had gone back to her husband. He had been wrong to hope for anything from them!

He looked at his watch again. Half past six. He did his best to master his uneasiness. The daily woman slammed a door to let him know she had arrived. They had got rid of the maid, and were thinking of leaving this apartment in order to "live on a smaller scale", as Mme Fonsèque had once said.

He turned his head towards the window. Rain was falling, running slow and oily down the window panes. The room was dark. He must put a light on, try to read. He switched on the light and picked a book up from his bedside table. There was a spot of ink on the turned-over hem of the sheet.

Marie-Claude did not come in until seven. He summoned her to his room at once, and she came in, hat in hand, cheeks flushed with the cold. Her face looked strangely young and healthy above her body, swamped in black mourning.

139

"You're late home today!"

"Oh, I went to the Ornamental Arts library with Totote Rouchez. How are you feeling?"

She came over to him and plumped up his pillows. She did not say anything, but he sniffed the scent of some secret satisfaction on her. He did not know what it was, and that irritated him. What was going on in the private world of her flesh and her spirit? On what paltry secret was the child's existence feeding? "What time will you be home tomorrow?" he asked.

"Well, not before seven."

He started with surprise. "Why not?"

Apparently she had promised Totote Rouchez to go to the Bibliothèque Sainte-Geneviève with her, and it would be difficult to say no now.

This all sounded perfectly likely, but the fear of deception poisoned Gérard's mind. She was lying. He knew that from the way her eyes slid to the right and slightly above his bed, from her careful tone of voice, the way she held her hands, spreading them slightly in the air in front of her as if placing them on the strings of an invisible harp. So many little details that combined to create an atmosphere of falsehood about her, conflicting with her ordinary words and gestures. But no sooner had he entertained these doubts than lucidity returned, removing them again. He concentrated on his role of cheerful and sublime resignation, for her benefit.

"You're quite right," he said pathetically. "You *should* go out, see your friends, look at works of art, have as good a time as you possibly can. You mustn't worry about me. Invalids are such a nuisance!"

Marie-Claude assured him it was only her lectures, and the work she had to do for her forthcoming examination, that prevented her from spending as much time with him as she would like to.

"Yes, that's just what I mean. You still think of me far too much. Honestly, I can manage quite well without you. I lie here with the memory of Mother, a few books, some paper, a pen . . . after all, I must get accustomed to being quite alone."

"You're not quite alone!"

"Not now, no—but I shall be! Remember what Mother used to say? 'Our children aren't made to devote themselves to us!' You'll be happy to leave me for the man of your choice some day."

She blushed suddenly, and moved away from Gérard. "What on earth do you mean?"

"Nothing wrong, for goodness' sake! I'm talking about your marriage."

"Even if I *do* get married some day I'll still see you!"

He smiled like a man obsessed and shook his head. "It won't be the same! I'll only be your guest, maybe even the spectre at the feast . . ."

She was nervously crumpling up a handkerchief, rolling it between the palms of her hands. "Gérard, you're being perfectly ridiculous! I can't see any point in this conversation."

He took her wrists, pulled her close to him, made her sit down on the edge of his bed, and went on, speaking into her ear in tones of violent affection. "Marie-Claude, you're much too good. You sacrifice yourself unthinkingly to people like me who need your love. You should be more selfish!"

He was watching her, and felt she was trembling, tense and shamefaced under his dominating gaze.

"Listen," she faltered, "I'll try to get home directly after the lecture tomorrow! I'll fix things with Totote . . ."

He stroked the nape of her neck with his sweating hand. "My dear, you must do exactly as you like. I don't want to force you to do anything. Now, off you go to wash your hands, and we'll have dinner together in here."

141

III

Vigneral was now coming to meet Marie-Claude from her lectures several times a week. She would manage to be first out of the hall, where a crowd of chattering, scented girls were preening and powdering their noses among the rows of seats. Vigneral took her walking along the misty embankments; they looked at the reflections of gas lamps in the calm dark water, like mooring-posts of light. They crossed the Pont des Arts and ended up in their usual haunt, a tearoom at the end of an alleyway full of stamp dealers and specialized bookshops. The tables had velour-covered partitions between them, and once the waitress was over by the cash register they could kiss without much risk of being seen.

Sometimes Marie-Claude would skip a boring lecture, and they would spend the afternoon in a box for two in a suburban cinema. The auditorium around them would be almost empty, with only a few pairs of heads, close together, to break the regular, swelling line of the seat backs. Soft music played, and the screen diffused gentle light (they hated outdoor scenes, or moments when newspaper articles or anonymous letters came on to the screen, because it meant the lighting was brighter). The box usually smelled of humbugs, dust and air freshener. The usherette's torch swayed down the rows of seats like a ship's porthole. They would hear whispering and the sound of chairs being pushed back in the box next to theirs. Marie-Claude would take off her hat, undo her coat, and fall into Vigneral's arms, while he embraced her fervently. He ran his skilled hands over her; he soon managed to unbutton the side of her dress, slip the strap of her petticoat off her shoulder, cup one breast, hold it, warm it, caress it tenderly until she moaned with pleasure. She was afraid of him at these moments, because she thought his face with its open mouth and glazed eyes looked unhappy in the

142

dim light, as if she were making him suffer at the same time as she abandoned herself to him. Then he would smile suddenly and draw her into the crook of his shoulder, nursing her like a little girl and speaking into her ear. She would put one hand under her cheek, so as not to leave face-powder on his jacket. An invisible orchestra played melting, sensuous music, inky lips came together on the screen. Marie-Claude's heart was full of melody and excitement; she felt the whole world was approaching the peak of perfection. "I love you, I love you," she murmured, just for the pleasure of saying it. And Vigneral would pull her close to him again, his fingers sliding over her stomach and thighs, urgently searching for her bare skin. She would go quite crazy, her head rocking from side to side as her bag fell to the floor.

They used to leave before the end of the main film. She would repair her face in the foyer mirror, which was surrounded by photographs of film stars. She saw pink blotches on her face, and her eyes looked small and sad. The ends of Vigneral's detachable collar would be curling, and his slightly swollen lip made him look like a naughty schoolboy. The girl selling tickets in the kiosk would yawn, widely, as slow rain fell outside, beyond the neon strip lighting. And Marie-Claude suddenly remembered that she ought not to have gone out to the cinema, because she was in mourning, and Gérard was alone at home waiting for her, and she was an unmarried girl . . .

She would go home feeling edgy and melancholy, and Gérard would immediately question her: where had she been, what time did the lecture finish? She had to lie. And even as she made her excuses, she could sense his cold, calm and predatory eyes on her face, her hands, her dress. She was afraid he might notice a trace of lipstick that had strayed to her chin, or the crumpled collar of her dress. She felt as if her love blazed around her, marking her out with a halo. To be honest, she was vaguely ashamed of being so happy when she was face to face with her sick, lonely brother. She told herself she ought not to have left him alone all afternoon. The long-

143

suffering kindness with which Gérard accepted his solitude made her feel worse than ever. He positively encouraged her to amuse herself, forget him, forget her grief for her mother. He suggested ideas of the probable future awaiting him without her, a desert of loneliness, a living death—but still, it would be enough for him to know *she* was happy! "Why, I've already managed without you, somehow, for a whole day," he would say, in the cheerful tones of a willing victim, so that Marie-Claude found it hard not to shed tears. She told herself she was very selfish, and set herself harsh penances: she would go two weeks, a month without seeing Vigneral.

Thus chastened, she would spend a few hours of total devotion with her brother, only to let herself go astray again the next day. Vigneral would see her come out of her lecture looking tired, as if she had slept badly, she would tell him her trouble, and he would comfort her in words so simple she was surprised to find how much they touched her.

No woman Vigneral had ever known had been able to give him such an impression of trusting and total submission. He had always had to fence with his mistresses. But Marie-Claude's vulnerability called forth his protective instincts. He felt he wanted to kiss her till her lips bled, and then rock her asleep like a big brother.

Their frenzied meetings in cinemas and cafés, their desperate, repetitive kissing, their unsatisfactory embraces were all aggravating his desire for her. He often dreamed of a locked room with a big bed in it, its covers thrown back in the dim light, and Marie-Claude lying on them naked, graceful, child-like, offered to him so that he could finally quench the vast thirst that consumed him. But her very confidence in him stopped him putting this notion into practice. Sometimes he thought it would be best to marry her, but his horror of that legitimized union immediately did away with any such fleeting impulse. He had broken off his relationship with Tina, and he cursed the stupid scruples which still kept him from sleeping with Maria-Claude. He told himself he must not see her any more, and then was angry if she cancelled a meeting. He tried not to love her. He felt jealous of her love for her brother. He sold less carbon paper than ever, and neglected his family. And one day he made up his mind to propose to her.

He borrowed a room from one of his bachelor friends for the occasion. The docile Marie-Claude went there with him. It was full of modern furniture battered around the edges, varnish chipped. The brown velour of the sofa was marked with pale, bare patches. There were photographs of women on the mantelpiece, and champagne glasses kept in a pouch-table. The place had a strong smell of brilliantine and tobacco.

In his mind, Vigneral went through the form of words he had devised for his proposal of marriage, but he could not bring himself to utter it. This was the first time he had been alone with her in a safe and comfortable room, and the temptation was too great. I'll marry her *afterwards* he thought.

She had put two black-bound exercise books down on the corner shelf of the room, and this little academic detail delighted him. He came over to her, pulled her down on the sofa, and they lay there together. She let him undress her, lying there still and shivering. She made no protest. He avoided looking at her face, in which her green eyes seemed to be fixed in mingled shame and pleasure.

When she was quite naked, he drank in the picture of her body: it was rather thin, and an appetizing honey-blonde. She lay with one leg stretched out and the other bent, knee in the air. Her slender, outspread arms revealed the vulnerable blue of her veins. Her breasts were small, round and firm, set well apart, with pink little girlish nipples. Whenever she breathed, her ribs stretched her skin. The fleece of hair below her flat belly was dark chestnut.

As Vigneral leaned over her, he saw that her toenails were varnished red. This observation, for no particular reason, removed the last of his scruples.

145

IV

A table had been brought to Gérard's bedside so that brother and sister could have their lunch together. Gérard was sitting up in bed with an old fringed rug round his shoulders. Dark stubble covered his cheeks, and his untidy black hair fell down the back of his neck and round his ears. Marie-Claude, face freshly made up, was sitting opposite him, busy eating an overdone mutton chop. She said she was in a hurry. Totote Rouchez was expecting her at two-thirty.

Irritated by her evident desire to get away from him, and sensing that she was lying, Gérard set about spending as long as he could over masticating the rather nasty vegetable soup which was his invalid meal. Marie-Claude had put her knife and fork down and was looking at her watch.

"Oh dear, you're bored," said Gérard, pleasantly. "I'm afraid I *do* eat slowly, but the doctor told me to make sure I chewed everything thoroughly—and I don't feel so bad about making you a little late since you haven't got a lecture today! Totote will understand. By the way, I'd love to meet Totote some time."

He reached for the bottle of Vichy water, filled his glass and drank, sipping slowly. He never took his eyes off Marie-Claude.

There were a few pieces of chicory left at the bottom of the dish. He was not eating them, he kept dabbing his mouth with his rolled-up napkin, sighing, and passing a hand over his eyes. Marie-Claude was thinking of Vigneral, who would be waiting for her at the exit from the Métro by now. But she dared not leave until Gérard had finished his lunch. "I think I *will* have a little more chicory," he said suddenly.

She went rigid with rage, and next moment was sorry for her impatience. He helped himself calmly, still talking.

"I'm getting a bit of appetite back. Oh, did I tell you I had a

146

note from Tellier? Apparently the baby's due in a fortnight. Well, Elisabeth's built all right for that sort of thing . . . don't you want any salad?"

"There's garlic in it."

"Well?" He had been very particular on this point the previous day, when he told the daily woman to put garlic in the salad dressing, for he was counting on it as a device to expose his sister. "Doesn't Totote like garlic, then?" he asked humorously.

Marie-Claude looked cross, blushed and shrugged her shoulders. How bad she was at this sort of thing! It might be that a few threats would be enough to make her confess all. But those brutal methods had failed with his other two sisters. He would be wily, play a clever game, and gradually poison the springs of her young love. He must keep her with him out of sympathy, not by force. He did not mind being pitied so long as she stayed with him! Every woman, he thought, has a secret wish to be a sacrificial victim. Well, he must make use of this itch for sacrifice, this desire to go to the stake, this slightly perverted and tainted caring instinct in Marie-Claude!

Oh yes, he'd soon get her into the state of high-minded renunciation in which she would do as he wanted. He would bring all his sores into play with a beggar's deliberate impudence, and would not be ashamed to accept the alms of her compassion. He would triumph over her by being her victim—but what suffering might he yet have to endure before he won her back? It was very hard to see her sitting there all dressed up and scented for someone else's benefit.

She was getting impatient. So she was afraid of making this stranger wait, and the stranger was pacing up and down the street looking at his watch.

"Don't you want any more?" he asked.

"No, I'm not hungry."

He saw her standing there, ready to escape him, radiant, already flushed with love. Her looks had improved recently, although he could not actually have said what had changed. On what poor nourishment did the beauty of the female face

147

feed? On what paltry satisfactions was Marie-Claude spending her transitory radiance? "Those mourning clothes don't suit you, my dear," he said, with spiteful intent. "Suppose you want to go to a show, have some fun? That rig makes it rather tricky, doesn't it?"

She did not reply, suddenly very busy folding and rolling up her napkin.

"Well, run along now! You obviously can't wait to be off—and quite right, too! I'm not the most cheerful of companions, not since Mother died. Actually, I feel as if it would be a kind of sacrilege to be enjoying anything personally just now—but you wouldn't understand, and I'm very glad of that for your own sake. I want you to be happy, feel no obligation to anything, least of all to me . . ."

His own remarks moved him to the point of tears, and he observed Marie-Claude turning pale. She looked away from him. Suddenly she gave a sort of hiccup, snatched up her bag from the chair where it was lying, and rushed out into the corridor.

"Marie-Claude!" he called. "Marie-Claude!"

But the front door was already closing after her.

The daily woman cleared the table, swept the crumbs off it on to the floor, and went back to the kitchen. Gérard took a salicylate pill. He still could not bend his legs, but the pain in his shoulders had gone. Perhaps he would be able to go out in two or three weeks' time. Then he would follow Marie-Claude and take the pair of them by surprise. Then he would know where to strike.

She had only just left, and the whole apartment was already frozen in hostile slumber. He no longer felt safe lying in his book-lined and dimly-lit room. Marie-Claude had got away, was running down the street, meeting some man, clinging to his arm, pressing close to him, apologizing breathlessly for being late. "My brother kept me, you see, and I don't want him to know . . ."

He dared not imagine what might happen next. Instead, to soothe his exhausting jealousy, he went back to the past in his

148

mind: like the old women he had seen in the rue Saint-Antoine bending to pick up bits of wooden paving, he too bent to pick up handfuls of memories and warm himself by their fire. He remembered Marie-Claude as a child, in the days when he need not watch the impulses of her heart. He thought of the whole complex organism of women, the progressive awakening of desire in them, the sly onset of maturity, both outward and inward. A little girl is happy in the bosom of her family: innocent, unaware, with no one and nothing taking any notice of her—but only let her features lengthen a little and her figure grow firm, her breasts swell, and men will take an interest, start stalking her, seeing her as a prey to their taste. They call her into their territory, they pursue her, they possess her . . . How he hated such remarks as, "How old is she now, then? Sixteen? Why, she could be nineteen!" No holds barred now, and the girl herself seems delighted! She can't wait to enter the fray, give herself, suffer. She takes the first comer, by common consent refusing to see any flaws of ugliness or falsehood in him. She wants to love, and love quickly, never mind whom, never mind why, she simply wants to love with all her heart. The world, thought Gérard, is grotesque, it stinks, it is nauseating. How disgusting it is to think that after a visit of any length of time from a friend or a mistress, you have to open a window to air the room, because it smells! But no one seems to notice, no one minds. Men and women shamefully comply with what they can't avoid. Smells, physical needs and illness don't destroy sentiment; you close your eyes to them. A useful expression, that. All around him were closing their eyes. He sometimes felt he had not been given the necessary anaesthetic for the interminable operation of life, the anaesthetic that soothed other people's pain. He alone was wide awake, lucid, flesh and spirit fully aware. The least little touch made him shriek. Yes, what he needed in order to accept existence was that precious drug which apparently intoxicated his own kind and got them into the condition of brute beasts, the drug of love. Only love could make them endure such hideous things, cast them into an artificial sleep in the very midst of the world.

He remembered the evening he had been in the Toc-Toc Bar with Vigneral and Tina when he had held a woman's sinuous, scented, skilful body against his own. He had felt nothing but disgust. Well, he must resign himself to enduring those shocks other people scarcely noticed, enduring them again and again; he must resign himself to a lifetime of unhappiness.

It was getting dark. He was surprised to see hail beating gently against the window panes. Marie-Claude was lightly clad; she would be cold. In which case she would be ill, and then at least she wouldn't leave the apartment. Why should he bother about her? Did anyone bother about him? No, they did not; at this precise moment nobody at all was thinking of him. He felt this absence of thought as if the ground had suddenly given way beneath him. Suppose I dropped dead, he thought, instantly conjuring up a picture of yellow clay lashed by rain, of a muddy trench into which a coffin with ridiculous brass ornaments was being lowered.

A little later he thought of dragging himself to Marie-Claude's room. If he searched her papers, he might find something about her private life? He got his stiff legs out of bed and put his dressing-gown on. His limbs felt dreadfully weak; his head was swimming slightly. He would never have the strength to stand up and walk all the way to Marie-Claude's door. He looked sadly at his thin white feet in their shapeless slippers, and touched his sore knees. At last, making a sudden effort, he stood up. The pain was so sharp that he nearly cried out, and he leaned all his weight against the wall. However, he went on his way, clinging to the furniture, groaning, breathing hard, and wiping away the sweat that broke out on his forehead with his sleeve.

Once he reached Marie-Claude's room, he collapsed into an armchair by the table and waited for a while, eyes closed, hands to his heart like an actor acknowledging applause. Gradually the beating of his heart calmed down. He opened his eyes again. The clean, fresh smell of the room made him realize that his own needed airing.

There were several exercise books on Marie-Claude's desk, and a little toy dog, and leaflets about cruises organized by the Ecole du Louvre. He touched these objects, as if petting them. He could not bring himself to ransack the drawers. The open door of the room behind him was inhibiting. He saw a torn-up first-class Métro ticket lying in an ashtray with a motto on it. She went second class when she was on her own. With an abrupt gesture, he did open a drawer. It was stuffed with notebooks, pencils, erasers, photographs. He set to work at once. His shaking fingers picked up items of this childish treasure hoard, took them apart, searched them. He identified the writing on envelopes, leafed through old timetables, scrutinized the faces of people in photographs, read visiting cards. None of the names told him anything. The pointless search made him feel more impatient than ever. He picked up a writing block, and saw the words. "This is my diary", written on the first page. The next few sheets had been torn out.

He flung everything back and tried to open another drawer, but this one was locked. Gérard picked up a paper-knife, inserted it into the crack beside the catch as far as it would go, and pressed slowly. The lock suddenly gave way. More invitations, more notebooks. He recognized a note he himself had written to his sister when she went away to stay with a girl friend for a fortnight in the holidays, a photograph of Mme Fonsèque, some First Communion pictures. He laid hands on these pathetic girlish secrets with the surreptitious haste of a thief. He was breathing hard, and sweating so much that his pyjamas had stuck to his shoulders.

He thought he heard footsteps, but they were on the floor above. The daily woman was tidying up the kitchen. Marie-Claude would not be back until seven. He did not know if he were pleased or sorry to have found any evidence against her. But this fruitless search did not lull his suspicions. She *was* seeing some man, he knew she was! He could sense it. But

151

who was it? One of his own friends? Lequesne was in England, Vigneral had a mistress, Hurault . . . no, it was more likely to be a fellow pupil at the Ecole du Louvre, some dim, pimply, pretentious student who dazzled her with phrases picked up from books on art. And she would leave him, Gérard, for someone like that, deceive him for someone like that!

He closed the drawer again, pressing the paper-knife down hard so that the catch would fall back into place. Then he went over to Marie-Claude's bed. From there, he could open her wardrobe. Dresses hung in it: dresses in light colours which she was not wearing now because she was in mourning. The thin hangers made them look as if they had skeleton shoulders inside them. Higher up, she kept piles of underwear on shelves lined with white paper. There was a faint smell of soap and skin cream—the smell that someone else, someone beside her, was breathing in at this moment. Her little bottles, her brush and comb stood on the mantelpiece. He wanted to destroy everything, fling them about the room. He put out his hand and touched her powder bowl, took its lid off, and for no special reason dipped his finger in the powder. Then he put the bowl back in place and began rubbing his powdery palms together. He felt crushed by indefinable distress and lassitude. He could have wished his sister was ugly, or feeble-minded, so that she could devote herself entirely to him. But would he have loved her then?

He fell across the bed, his face buried in the counterpane. What was he doing here? What was he waiting for? His eyes were very close to the big rose-pattern of the counterpane's fabric. There was a faint noise in his ears, like the sizzling of fat in a pan. Over ten minutes passed before he raised his head. His shoulders and knees hurt. He moaned softly to break the silence.

At last he went back to his room, feeling his way along the walls. He saw Marie-Claude's crumpled handkerchief on the chair by his bed; he lay down and dozed off, with his eyes on that white patch.

V

Marie-Claude had just gone out. Gérard was sitting in an armchair opposite his table, at work on a translation. He had been feeling better for the last few days. He could get up and walk about the apartment. Yesterday, Luce and Paul Aucoc had spent the whole afternoon with him. They were just back from Metz, where they had been visiting the Telliers. Elisabeth had given birth to a boy. "A lovely baby!" said Luce, a doting look in her eye. "Seven pounds! Elisabeth's up and about already—simply thrilled, of course! As for her husband, he's positively bursting with pride! It's quite embarrassing! They're calling him Philippe. Rather a dull name, don't you think?"

Gérard was surprised by his present indifference. The Aucocs' marriage was of no interest to him now. Let Luce expend her energy on the mutual intonations of her voice, her supple, cat-like movements and the rolling of her eyes as much as she liked—her brother had passed beyond that straightforward exasperation for which she used to provide fuel. Even Elisabeth's fate aroused no feelings in him but a bitterness that was close to boredom. Their lives were lived on a different planet, lived by people who were nothing to him, and whom he would never manage to understand. His own life was here with Marie-Claude, in Marie-Claude's shadow, in her warmth. He would die if anyone should think of taking his place. He needed her presence as he needed air itself. He would have liked her to be all his—but she was lavishing her time and her affection, maybe her caresses, on her secret daytime life. She would emerge from he knew not what murky ocean, with menace muttering in its depths. She would stand there in his doorway, shedding countless unfamiliar words and movements like waterdrops, and he would have to penetrate those misleading externals to find her again. He

153

pursued an ever elusive revelation over the sensitive surface of her face, in the pliant music of her voice. Who was the man to whom her mysterious afternoon expeditions were devoted? What did their meetings consist of? What did they expect of each other?

If only someone could have taken his mind off his obsession with the subject! Sometimes he thought Lequesne would have been able to understand him, but he had no news of his friend. Vigneral did not come to the apartment any more. Nobody did. And in his heart he liked it best that way.

He felt no inclination for anything these days. He had abandoned his essay on Evil. He was in a hurry to finish this translation; it would be his last, and then he would look for a job. Once Mme Fonsèque's four children had probate of her will, there would not be much between them. He and Marie-Claude would rent a smaller apartment, and he would live there with her as long as she liked. He shivered, as if feeling the wind of an abyss at his feet. In a week's time he would be able to go out. In a week's time he would be able to fight for his happiness.

He bent over the paper, upon which his pen had stopped moving, and re-read the last sentence. "Mrs Ploughman took the stopper out of the Chinese bottle in which she kept a decoction of colchicum seeds. As her husband turned his head to look at the blazing log fire . . ."

He crossed out what he had written, and leaned back in his chair. Like that husband looking at the fire, he thought, with someone distilling a mortal poison drop by drop, behind my back. Did Marie-Claude realize what torture she was inflicting on him? He wished he could feel more detached, disengaged, could feel superior, smile scornfully, but he was constantly devastated by his gusts of fury. "Mrs Ploughman took the stopper out of the Chinese bottle . . ."

He could see the sky through his window; it was pale blue. The fountains in the Place des Vosges were splashing softly. When he was a child the sound of them used to make him think of some desperate pursuit through the undergrowth of a weed. A man bearing off his prey into the heart of thickets wet with rain and full of green shade. And Gérard recognized the woman's happy face, but the face of the man kept changing like running water.

It was five o'clock. Pairs of lovers would soon turn up to haunt the arcades around the square. He had seen so many such couples lurking in the shadow of the columns, clinging close, grave and motionless like horses at a watering trough. His room was encircled by love, by kisses, by clandestine embraces. Once, he had not minded. Now he feared it, since Marie-Claude had joined that kissing, stroking twilight throng. She was on their side. He could almost have wished to be like other people himself, to have sudden carnal hungers, seek for easy satisfactions, lose and daze himself in the primitive joy of possession. Vigneral, for instance, did not suffer. Vigneral ate, drank, slept and loved, and food, drink, sleep and women were enough to calm any momentary uneasiness he felt. He would not allow himself suffering unless he knew where to find its cure. The moral serenity of the idiot. Perhaps Lequesne was right? Perhaps one should leave it to a superior power to play the game and win or lose it for us? Not always, of course, but sometimes, when fighting on one's own is too hard. Today, for instance, now . . . how sweet to be no more than a branch bending obediently to the wind, to be flowing water following the curve of the bank, to be a pebble on the road pushed about at random by passing feet.

Gérard put his hands, attentive as human faces, to his cheeks and his burning forehead. He felt he was teetering on the edge of an unknown domain, he sensed some indefinable change in himself. He was not quite sure that he was properly awake yet.

A ring at the doorbell brought him back from his thoughts.

It could not be Marie-Claude, and he was not expecting a visitor. The door opened, and closed again, and he heard the daily woman's slippers coming down the corridor.

"It's a lady to see you, Monsieur."

155

"A lady?"

It took him several seconds to recognize the woman standing in his doorway as Tina. She had her handbag clasped protectively to her stomach, an amazing black velvet hat trimmed with artificial feathers made of mottled cretonne weighed her head down, her face was painted, and she was wearing a blue beauty spot beside one eye.

She had put on a little weight, and was breathing fast and noisily.

"I don't suppose you were expecting to see me," she said, in tones of formal correctness. "And I hesitated for a long time before I decided to come. I mean, it's all so delicate, isn't it?"

She sat down, crossed her long legs and looked at the walls and the window, eyes slightly narrowed.

Gérard felt wary. This visit bothered him, because he could not imagine why the girl had come, and he dared not ask her straight out. However, he did inquire, "Who gave you my address?"

"Nobody—I was with you in the taxi, though, the one that took you home after our night out. So I remembered the building . . . I say, how funny you did look! Why didn't you ever come back to the Toc-Toc Bar? Had a good time, didn't we, the three of us? We could've done it again!"

She gave him a smile full of complicity, and then lowered her eyes to the toes of her shoes, which were pointed like the jaws of a pike. Her strong scent filled the room.

"You'll be wondering why I'm here, though," she went on. "Haven't you heard anything about it from your friend Vigneral?" She uttered these last three words with haughty contempt.

"Oh, I hardly see him nowadays."

"Then that makes two of us!"

She raised a finger with a long, sharp, red nail, and the few dark hairs remaining in her plucked eyebrows came together. "We're all washed up!" she announced. "Oh, no scenes, not even one little explanation! Didn't so much as bother to tell me, did he? Just stopped coming to see me one fine day. So a

156

week goes by, and then I get a note. 'I love you, but we must stop meeting.' Okay. Fine. Only I've left my job on account of him. 'I earn enough for two, with what my parents give me,' he told me. He didn't want me working. He had me rent a two-roomed flat. So how am I going to pay the rent now? If I'd known in advance I'd have been more careful, but—well, you know how it is with these things! You can never tell when something like that's going to get up and hit you, if you ask me. Oh, Monsieur Gérard, can't you do anything for me? Bring influence to bear on him? I'm not asking him to start seeing me again, that'd be too much to expect, but he might at least give me enough to get by on for a few weeks. I don't suppose he *wants* me dying of starvation just because of his whims and fancies!"

She dabbed the end of her nose with a pale green, gauzy handkerchief.

"The moment I mentioned you to him he'd stop listening," said Gérard. "Why don't you go and see him at home?"

"He wouldn't let me in!"

"Well, write to him."

"He wouldn't answer—no, Monsieur Gérard, you must, *must* do this for me! I haven't got any money, I haven't got a job, I came here on foot to save the Métro fare. I'm telling you all this because I know you'll understand. You're not like that brute—he doesn't think of anything but his appetites! You seem so kind and serious and honest! Surely you won't refuse to give me a little help?" She began sniffling quietly, her shoulders rising and falling in time. "He told me you'd got a shop," she went on. "Maybe, just for the time being—"

"We've sold it."

"Can you think of anything else?"

"Well, no . . . but if I do happen to hear of something . . ."

"Oh, don't say that!" she cried. "That's what people always say when they want to get rid of you! *You* don't want to get rid of me, do you, Gérard? I'm so lonely! I'm so unhappy!"

She blinked hard, to start the tears coming, and quite soon the ends of her eyelashes were shining damply. She bit her heavily painted lips and wrung her hands. A laboured sob racked out.

"Oh, Gérard, Gérard," she moaned, adding hoarsely, "Oh, whatever will you think of me?"

Gérard did not like the way things were going in the least. He was unsure of whether to offer her a glass of water, money, or good advice. "Please," he faltered, "please . . ."

"Oh dear, I'm so ashamed!" Tina sighed.

And taking off her hat, she threw it on the bed. She shook out her black hair, which was shiny and supple as silk, and thrust her small hands into it in a gesture of calculated despair. Gérard came over to her.

"Listen, I promise I'll do everything I can . . ." he said.

She raised her pretty painted face to his, her eyes wet, her lips parted, as she had raised it when he was dancing with her in the nightclub.

"Oh, yes! Oh, yes!" she murmured, with a tender, docile look. Suddenly she took his wrist. "Here—sit down beside me!"

He pulled up a chair with his free hand.

"Oh, it does me good to see you!" she went on. "I liked you the very first evening we met, but I didn't dare tell you, even though I wanted to, because of you-know-who! He was so jealous! Well, I can make up for it now—would you like that?"

Another man would have risen to his feet, taken her in his arms, and used her like an animal. That was all she expected. That was all she asked for. That was the only way she knew of getting a little money, or a job. He got up.

"Oh, my heart—it's beating so fast! I shall suffocate!" she said.

He thought that he wished he could have desired her, as other men would. For various reasons he could not define, he felt one ought to sink to those muddy depths, that place of ruin and ravishment to which all his sisters had fled. But he had a headache. His hand, held between Tina's, was becoming damp; he was ashamed of that, just as he was

158

ashamed of his unshaven face, his greasy nose, and the broken spot on his forehead. Tina laid his hands on her breast.

"Feel that—can you feel my heart beating now?"

They faced each other in watchful silence. Gérard, in an attempt to arouse his desire, reminded himself of various items of erotic literature. He owned an illustrated edition of Casanova's *Memoirs*. One of the engravings was of a naked woman seated astride a chair, hands spread over her breasts like starfish. She was wearing a black mask with a little veil falling to just below her chin. There was no hairy shadow to emphasize the plump slope of her mount of Venus.

Tina stood up too, pressing close to him. He felt her sturdy body against his own, knew it would respond to any invitation. She clasped him in her arms and raised her lips to him. He felt quite cold, and ridiculous. He could have wept. Suddenly, he recalled the quarter-carcase of a bullock he had seen the young man unloading outside the butcher's shop in rue Saint-Antoine, the great lump of bloodless meat clinging to the man, lolling about him like a fat and amorous woman. He closed his eyes, sick at heart, feeling nothing. Tina's tongue briskly caressed his own. He felt as if he were eating something disgusting. He wanted to draw back, spit out that rubbery object stopping up his mouth. Circles of fire were exploding in his brain. He had a close view of the flesh of a stranger's face: open pores, long eyelashes, and the eyes of an honest working woman. Despite himself, he breathed in the warm, musky, odour of a brunette. She was doing her best. She was surprised at her inability to arouse his sickly body with her own. She moaned, conscientiously, "Oh, oh!"

It reminded him of the time when Marie-Claude had 'flu and had to have her throat painted.

"Oh, now!" she cried, falling backwards on the bed, her skirt up to her knees.

Gérard thought of the three black figures in the cemetery, a wanton gust of wind lifting their dresses beside the grave. He did not want to think of his sisters now, but a grotesque kind of obsession set the three of them between this woman and

159

himself. Trying to pull himself together, he murmured a quotation, foolishly:

> ". . . in the plain array
> Of Beauty snatched from quiet sleep away."

"Undo me down the back," said Tina.

She pulled her dress quickly down to her waist, and slipped off the shoulder straps of her petticoat. Startled, Gérard looked at her pale, round commonplace breasts. Her nipples were brown and crumpled. He noticed a mole with a long hair growing from it near the right nipple. I am looking at flesh that Vigneral has caressed, he thought. He was happy the day she first gave herself to him. Almost any man would be happy to be in my shoes now . . .

She held out her arms to him, and kissed his mouth again. He thought he smelled tobacco and food in the kiss, as once before. A spasm of fear and disgust shook him. He felt as if he were falling from the top of a tower into space, and almost cried out.

Suddenly she was chanting, "Don't worry, don't worry, it'll be all right . . ."

And instantly he remembered that room in the brothel, and the plump, pale woman encouraging him in an undertone.

"Leave me alone! Get out of here!" he shouted. He was gasping, as if he had been weeping violently.

She adjusted her clothes, looking pale and surprised. "What is it? What's the matter?"

He had buried his face in his hands, overwhelmed by an infinite sense of shame. "Go away!" he muttered, bleakly. "Go away!"

She stood up, eyes flashing, jaw set . "Throwing me out, eh?"

"Yes . . . yes! Go away!"

"Oh, you bastard—you're a right little bastard! I suppose you're in this too, along with your fine friend! You *want* him to give me the push and marry your sister! And I was fool

160

enough to come to you for help . . . huh! I see it all now! Only too well!"

"What do you mean?"

"Mean to say you didn't know, you slimy bastard? He's been after her for months! When he left me, he told me he was leaving me for her! But if you think he's going to make an honest woman of her you've got another think coming!"

Gérard was stunned, every thought driven out of his head. The ground seemed to be shaking beneath his feet. The ceiling was coming down to crush him. He was breathing so fast he thought his chest would burst. He seized Tina's shoulders with extraordinary force, pulled her close to him, and shouted, "You're lying! You're lying!" into her face, spitting out the words.

She jerked free and began to laugh. "It's no good now, sweetie! You can just let me go!"

"No—wait! Stay here—tell me—"

"Stay here? No, thanks! Wouldn't want to tire you out, would we, Don Juan?"

She had gone to the door, and was fastidiously wiping her hands on her thin handkerchief.

"How you sweat!" she said. "It's all over my fingers. You're ugly. Your breath smells. You couldn't make a living soul fancy you—and you can't even get it up either! I guess I don't bear you any grudge, I feel sorry for you, that's what!"

He did not move. He was not listening to her. He did not notice when she left the room.

When Marie-Claude came home, she found Gérard scanning a railway timetable.

"I'm feeling better," he told her curtly. "We're going away tomorrow, you and I, to spend a few days with Elisabeth."

Peering over the timetable, he saw the expression of panic on his sister's face.

VI

The cradle occupied the centre of the room. Gérard saw a spherical piece of shrivelled, wrinkled meat emerging from a mound of pink blankets and lace. Its nose was as shapeless as an earlobe, its lips dribbled. Marie-Claude instantly clapped her hands, uttered a cry of delight, and bent over the baby to devour it with her eyes, making smiling faces at it. She thought her nephew looked like Elisabeth. Elisabeth said he was the image of her husband. "I've got a photograph of Joseph at that age, and the likeness is really strking!"

She was paler and thinner, but there was a new softness in her eyes, and even her features seemed to have relaxed tenderly.

Gérard looked at her empty belly, its burden gone, ready to accept another. He imagined the baby's birth, his sister lying spreadeagled and bleeding, offering her naked body to the midwife's quick hands, letting them drag out this bald little monster, with its face that might have been made of superimposed fingers, while she cried out, loud and long. These sordid images of torture turned his stomach.

He sat down in an armchair near the door. The train journey had tired him. It had been unwise to come at all, since the doctor had told him, at the beginning of the week, that he ought not to go out yet. But it was a matter of urgency to get Marie-Claude away from Vigneral. If this first separation were followed by another, in the summer holidays, it might quench their ardour and allow Vigneral to set about some other conquest. And Marie-Claude had agreed to go away with her brother without protesting. Did she guess he knew? Did she suspect the real reason for their departure from Paris?

"Well, what do you think of the son and heir, Gérard?" Tellier was clapping him on the shoulder.

"Men can never see anything in children of that age," said

Elisabeth.

"I beg to differ!" Tellier protested.

"Oh, it's different for you—you're his father!"

He objected, claiming that it was fascinating from the "psychological point of view", anyway, to watch instinct develop in a baby, that there was "a certain moral beauty" about a child only a few days after birth, and that babies in general provided "much food for thought".

Elisabeth interrupted all this: it was the baby's bathtime, and the whole family went into the bathroom. Elisabeth put on a white smock, unfolded a table with an oilcloth cover, and set about unwrapping the baby, who struggled, squalled, and spat out transparent globs of saliva.

When he was naked, the adult heads all came together to examine this roll of pink flesh with its bulging stomach and protruding navel. The baby was still yelling, splayed hands like little crabs reaching up to the light.

Elisabeth picked him up, held him over a bowl of water, and washed him with brisk, efficient movements, while Marie-Claude said delightedly that he was "an absolute poppet!" and Tellier remarked that, "That lad has no idea of the honour we adults are doing him, watching him have his bath!" When he had been wiped down and patted dry, Elisabeth powdered him under the armpits and on the bottom with talcum powder, parting the rolypoly legs with one finger and shaking the tin of talc over his thighs and his tiny, limp penis, which lay there looking like some tender morsel.

Gérard struggled against the revulsion rising within him. The exhibition of this miniature male nude to all eyes seemed to him improper. It was bound to put slightly indecent thoughts into his two sisters' heads—especially Marie-Claude's. She was overcome by delight at all this intimate fiddling about.

"Oh, look at his dear little hands and his dear little feet!" she cried, dropping a kiss on them. She sat beside Elisabeth to watch her give "Master Philippe" his bottle. The baby sucked greedily at the teat, and then abruptly stopped. There was general consternation. Tellier wondered if it was wind, and suggested pinching his nose to make him open his mouth. Elisabeth thought the bottle wasn't warm enough. Tellier swore he had been very careful to get the temperature right. At this point a slight burp was heard, Elisabeth put the teat back between the baby's lips, and the level of the liquid in the bottle went gently down, along with the spectators' concern. When there were only a few drops left, the tiny face creased and went red, and its mouth opened to bring up a whitish liquid, which Tellier promptly mopped up with his handkerchief.

"You mustn't do that!" cried Elisabeth. "Your handkerchief might be dirty!"

Wincing, Gérard turned his head away. He was sick of the sight of those ludicrous figures of covetousness and stupidity, bending over the cradle as if it were a feeding trough. The very air he breathed had a disgusting smell of baby, sour milk and talcum powder. He felt he would not be able to eat any dinner.

Dinner-time conversation was strictly limited to the subject of child-rearing. It was all about weight records, the ideal teat for a bottle, and how the baby "did his business".

Elisabeth and Marie-Claude seemed to be fascinated by these sordid details. They talked a lot. They ate a lot.

During dessert, Tellier told slightly improper stories which made them burst out laughing, their napkins to their mouths. Elisabeth looked at her husband with wifely affection and held his hand under the tablecloth. Gérard would hardly have known his sister, once so reserved, remote and intelligent, in the woman she now was: weakened by vulgar happiness, firmly entrenched in the narrow satisfactions of maternity. He hated the fact that he could guess at the unclean contentment of marriage, with what he assumed to be the acceptance of promiscuity, personal habits, smells and secretions, behind every move the Telliers made. Theirs was a universe of dirty linen, full chamber pots and disgusting needs, now revealed to him, and he alone understood the horror of it. He claimed to

164

be tired after the long journey, to excuse his silence, and everyone believed him, since no one was taking any interest in him.

"We're going to bed very early," said Elisabeth. "I'll make up Gérard's bed in the dining room once the table's cleared, and you're sleeping in what will be Philippe's nursery, Marie-Claude!".

So they still had the baby in their own room. They kissed and made love beside its cradle. Now and then their embraces must be interrupted by a wail. He imagined Elisabeth reluctantly withdrawing from Tellier's clasp, getting up still sweating and excited and flustered, to lean over the crying baby. "It's nothing much!" She would change the wet nappy, and then go back to her husband where he waited impatiently between the sheets.

It was a long time before Gérard could get to sleep in the strange room. He looked at the big, polished table, the chairs standing against the wall as if they were in a waiting room, the bow-fronted sideboard with items of cut glass on it. He heard faint sounds elsewhere in the apartment, tried vainly to make out gasps and the noise of bare feet on the floor. His mind was working feverishly.

The baby was one more barrier between Elisabeth and her brother. Its birth meant that the last link between them, already a weak one, had just broken. You can take a woman away from her husband, but not from her child. It was terrible to think of a similar fate awaiting Marie-Claude, to think that she hoped for it, was looking forward to it in the most idiotic detail. At this very moment, no doubt, she was thinking of Vigneral, feeling sorry she was not his wife and had not got a child of his to bath, as Elisabeth bathed her own flabby, plucked infant.

Gérard could not imagine what Marie-Claude saw in his friend. Vigneral, though tall and strong, had a red neck and red ears; Vigneral was stupid and conceited and had no strength of character at all. But just as bitches pick up the scent of another dog on a visiting stranger and will follow him

165

about, fawning on him until he pats them, Marie-Claude picked up the scent of interesting affairs on Vigneral and unthinkingly let him charm her with that spell. Vigneral himself didn't deny that his success with women was due to his reputation. "They just fall into my lap—they stun me, they devour me, and I can't do without them! There was Solange, for instance . . ." To whom was he confiding his flirtation with Marie-Claude? He was certainly telling someone. Half the pleasure he got from a love affair was in the stories he told about it, embellished by scabrous details, cynical remarks, and the coarse laughter of a horse-dealer. Why had he taken Marie-Claude away from Gérard? He didn't love her. He had no intention of marrying her, or sleeping with her. He had no right to treat his friend's sister like other girls. This hunt was crueller than any of the others. It was an insult to their friendship, a betrayal, a low-down trick! It cried out for vengeance!

Sitting up in bed, Gérard quite surprised himself by his hatred, no longer a sentiment but a sensation, nagging at him, literally choking him in its malevolent grasp. He tried reasoning with himself. Marie-Claude wasn't really in love with Vigneral, or she would have refused to leave Paris. It was just a flirtation, not real passion. Immediately, however, he answered himself back: flirtation or passion, she was not thinking of *him* any more. This, and this alone, was what tormented him: the gradual withdrawal of affection and admiration from him, the ebbing of the tidal waters in which he had lived, leaving nothing but a sandy desert with a few puddles and lifeless shells scattered about it.

A clock struck three, gently, and another clock somewhere in the building answered it. Gérard put out his hand and touched his knees under the bedclothes. His joints hardly hurt any more, but he was still very weak. Perhaps that accounted for his failure to respond to Tina? He was a convalescent. He was undernourished. But why look for excuses? He thought of her voice as she snapped, "Wouldn't want to tire you out, would we, Don Juan?" And of the movement with which she bared her round, white breasts with their large nipples.

It was hot in the room, and the smell of dinner still lingered there. Gérard got out of bed and opened the window.

Sleeping buildings stood on either side of the road, under a wide, dark sky with pale clouds piled in it like cotton waste.

He heard the sound of carts coming from the nearby barracks; no doubt some regiment or other was setting out on manoeuvres. The rattle of the wheels came closer as the carts turned the corner of the road. The head of the detachment came into sight. The horses were walking along, still drowsy, heads bowed. The cannon jolted over the cobblestones with a heavy, iron sound. The tin hats of the drivers and the gun crews shone faintly in the dark. They looked up as they passed the open window. No doubt they envied him, the unknown occupant of a comfortable room watching them file past, fuddled with sleep and tedium, shaken about like so many sacks, off to carry out any number of ridiculous tasks. If only they knew how much *he* envied *them!* He was the unhappiest man in the world! Not that anybody knew, or cared.

The detachment moved away in a dim, mediaeval light, a van with an orange lantern on it brought up the rear. A train whistled. The station was not far off. Gérard remembered their arrival, in a taxi. The taxi had driven over a big iron bridge, and he had been able to see the wide area below, where a network of rails reached to the horizon. Red and green lights winked on in the dusk, engines manoeuvred, spewing out dense jets of steam. The sight was reminiscent of a human brain, with its tangle of tracks, its contradictory signals, and all its puffings and pantings. Ideas too go along side by side without collision, obey the rules of shunting, make for their terminus and stop to unload themselves, having run out of steam. He closed his eyes; the noise and lights of the railway station were there inside his head. Arrivals and departures, the melancholy and deserted platforms. He thought he would never get to sleep.

He woke up late in the morning. He could hear Marie-Claude's voice in the nearby bathroom.

167

"Celina, be my wife,
I'll love you all my life . . ."

She was singing. She was singing as she washed.

* * *

The week that followed was a week of continual torture for
Gérard. Tellier spent the day at the office and did not come
home until seven, but even when he was out Gérard could not
have as much of his sisters' company as he would have liked.
Elisabeth and Marie-Claude never left the baby's side, talked
of nothing else. There seemed to be a new bond of friendship
between them, and it infuriated Gérard. He was, in fact,
jealous of their good understanding, their laughter, their
interminable low-voiced confabulations. Sometimes they
would stop in mid-sentence when he came into the room, and
when they resumed their conversation he fancied they had
changed the subject. He felt left out, excluded from their
confidence and affection, and he was afraid. At such moments
he would go out for a walk in the town, and people would
turn to look at him: a young man walking along at an old
man's shuffling pace, leaning on a stick and stopping to get
his breath back.

The streets were full of soldiers. They invaded the café
terraces, the places of entertainment, the alleys of the
Esplanade. Gérard went down to the Boulevard Poincaré and
walked to the belvedere above the Moselle. He stayed there
for some time, breathing the acrid river air, watching green
shadows like snakes moving on the water.

Night was falling. Cold air wafted up to him from the river.
Gérard thought of going back. He felt he could no longer bear
the company of Tellier, Elisabeth and Marie-Claude, sitting
round that table amidst the clatter of spoons and the smell of
soup, and interminably discussing the baby. What was he
doing here, with people who no longer cared for him? What
did he hope for, from people who were so selfishly concerned

168

with themselves? He would go back to Paris alone, summon Vigneral to come and see him, and persuade him to stop pursuing Marie-Claude. Once that was settled he would get Marie-Claude to come back too and have her all to himself.

He was dreaming of this triumphant outcome as he climbed the steps leading to the Esplanade. The sky was a very soft blue, and bands were playing in the nearby cafés. He felt an extraordinary beatitude, as if he had sensed that beyond his present difficulties there lay a universe of calm and love which was not closed to him.

VII

The day after he got back to Paris, Gérard received a long letter from Marie-Claude. She was writing to say that Vigneral had asked her to marry him, and she had decided to accept him. Elisabeth thought she should, too. There followed a lyrical outpouring, all about Vigneral's sterling qualities of heart and mind and the blissful future awaiting them once they were married. She was so glad, she said, that the man who loved her was such a good friend of her brother's! It wouldn't be like having a stranger in the family; her future husband was someone Gérard knew and liked already. "He thinks very highly of you, and we often talk of you."

Elisabeth had added a few lines saying that she thought the marriage so desirable, she couldn't imagine Gérard's feeling otherwise, and so, at her suggestion, Marie-Claude was sending Vigneral, who was "fretting with impatience in Paris", a telegram giving him the "good news".

Such hypocrisy disgusted Gérard. Marie-Claude had been afraid to tell him her plans to his face! She had waited until they were apart, and then enlisted Elisabeth in her cause and got her to strike the blow. Perhaps she had agreed to go away in the first place only in the hope of the good her brother's unsuccessful manoeuvre might do her? She was probably afraid that if she had dared to mention her marriage to him in person, he would have put his foot down straight away—squashed the idea and talked her out of it. So she preferred to stab him in the back, without warning, out of the blue. And Elisabeth, bearing him a grudge for his victories over her, had guided her hand.

Gérard was shattered by the news. He spent a whole day consumed with hatred for his sisters and devising cunning means of revenge. He had not spoken his last word yet! He could still strike back. And that same evening he wrote to

170

Vigneral by express post, asking him to come and see him. If he could not get at Marie-Claude directly, he could get at the man she loved. Countless arguments sprang to his mind, and he lined them up with gleeful precision. Vigneral had no strength of character. He could soon deal with Vigneral! He, Gérard Fonsèque, would not be the man he was if he were to fail with so pathetic an opponent.

The express letter he had sent his friend fixed an appointment for three o'clock next day. By two-thirty Gérard was already getting impatient. He had sent the daily woman home. Despite his fatigue, he paced from room to room, lovingly going over the phrases which he intended to use in arguing with his friend. He had foreseen all possibilities: Vigneral might be ill at ease, and then he would point out that his lack of prospects and dissolute way of life should have forbidden him even to think of such a thing. Vigneral might be angry—he would confound him by quoting his own words at him, remarks he had once utterd to the effect that "if I ever marry anyone it'll just be to fill a gap between two affairs . . . marriage is for men too lazy for the chase, and I'm not one of that sort!" Vigneral might be emotional, in which case he would get at him by pointing out that Marie-Claude's happiness came first; was he sure he could make her happy! As her brother he, Gérard, must take leave to doubt it . . .

He would ask Vigneral into the drawing room and make him sit down in the armchair by the window, where his mother used to sit. He himself would remain standing while speaking to him, dominating him from above. He would begin quite calmly, but if the other man started to argue his own tone would rise, and he would shout angrily if need be.

Whatever happened, Vigneral was not going to leave the apartment without giving in to him.

Gérard went into the drawing room, checked the arrangement of the furniture and leafed through the photograph album lying on its shelf. The last few pages were full of pictures of the weddings of Luce and Elisabeth.

A little clock, flanked by unglazed white porcelain

ornaments, struck three. Gérard listened intently to all the footsteps coming up the stairs, but they always passed his floor. He was as nervous as if he were about to take an exam. He musn't forget anything. He mustn't lose his head. He took the copy of his express letter out of his pocket. Yes, he *had* said three o'clock. And he had underlined the words "a conversation of the utmost importance". Right. It was a hot day, but he was not going to open the window, in case anyone out in the square heard them shouting.

At three-thirty the doorbell rang. He froze. Then he went into the hall, weak at the knees, his breath coming short. He had not seen Vigneral since the day of his mother's funeral. He thought of his friend's lean, high-coloured face, his wolfish teeth, his pale, prominent eyes. Each detail he remembered fanned his fury. He opened the door. There stood Lequesne.

"You!" exclaimed Gérard.

The young man wore no hat or coat. His face looked thinner and his eyes larger and darker than before. He was smiling cheerfully.

Gérard stepped back.

"Hullo—I'm only passing through Paris," Lequesne told him. "I'm off back to London this evening—called to see you earlier this week, but you were away, and your *concierge* said . . ."

Stunned and furious, Gérard had no intention of letting him in.

"I say, is this a bad moment?"

It was indeed a bad moment! The very moment when Gérard could least do with him—he might have chosen it on purpose! He must get rid of Lequesne, thought Gérard, before Vigneral arrived.

"Were you working?" asked Lequesne.

"Yes . . . but actually, the thing is I'm expecting someone. Look, I can't stop and talk to you now—later, maybe? Say tomorrow . . ."

"I'll have left Paris tomorrow."

Gérard was panic-stricken. He might hear Vigneral's footsteps on the stairs any moment.

"You're leaving so soon? Well . . . well, that's too bad. I mean, if you'd only let me know . . ." His voice was rising, but seeing the surprise in his friend's face, he immediately apologized. "Sorry. I'm rather edgy just now. It's this very important interview. If I'm free later this afternoon . . ."

Although Lequesne could not know anything, Gérard felt as if his intentions had been guessed, understood and judged in silence. He felt sad, uneasy, devoid of any ideas.

"Well, look, my train leaves at seven-forty," said Lequesne. "Suppose I wait for you in the station buffet from six-thirty to seven-thirty?"

"Fine!" said Gérard. He wiped his hand on his trousers before offering it to Lequesne. And at that moment he heard rapid footsteps running upstairs.

"You must go!" cried Gérard. "You must go now!"

But Vigneral was already coming up the last few steps.

"Hullo, it's Lequesne!" he said. "I thought you were in America!"

"No, England!"

"Same thing as far as I'm concerned!" He turned briskly and seized Gérard by the shoulders. "Heard the news, have you? I bet you can't get over it! I can hardly get over it myself, come to that! He's told you about it, has he, Lequesne?"

"No."

"Take a deep breath, then! I'm getting married! And who am I getting married to? Three guesses! What, no offers? I'm getting married to Marie-Claude!"

He was laughing, triumphantly. He looked proud and confident.

"Staggered, eh? Better not congratulate me too soon, though—it's not all fixed yet, I suppose, seeing Gérard here has summoned me by express letter! He's about to ask me no end of searching questions about my state of health, venereal heredity, means of support, university diplomas, political opinions and expectations! And heaven help me if I fail to

173

pass the test! I dare say I'll be kept in after school—he's a terrible fellow, you know, is Gérard! Come on, then, old chap, open fire: 'Sir, before I entrust you with my sister's happiness, it is my duty to ask you for some enlightenment. There are nasty rumours going round about you, but I don't suppose you'll have any trouble in dispelling them!'"

Gérard was struck dumb. He had never imagined their conversation beginning in this grotesque way. Cast into increasing confusion, he recollected scraps of the phrases he had prepared. None of them fitted the circumstances. Losing his temper would make him look ridiculous. Going along with Vigneral's clowning would undermine his position in the game. Events had caught up with him, and overtaken him too.

Vigneral was still preening himself, magnificent in his easy, facetious manner. "Well, are you or aren't you going to interrogate me? I've got exactly twenty minutes, old chap! In twenty minutes' time I have to leap into a taxi and go to see a customer who's summoned me for quarter past four precisely—suspicious fellow, he is, one of your sort, has to have the goods personally delivered by hand! Two in one day is rather much. Never mind, I can take it!"

Gérard had gone quite pale. Shame and hatred made his jaw tremble, and drops of sweat were running down his forehead. "Look, I must have a serious word with you," he said, dully.

"Oh Lord! I knew it was all up with me!" exclaimed Vigneral, making a comical face.

Lequesne began to laugh. Gérard felt his own assurance melting away. His plans of attack had all assumed a Vigneral without substance, a phantom, a creature of his own imagination. Faced with a being of flesh and blood, he found all his advance preparations were illusory. He saw himself cutting a pitiful, distraught figure in front of the man he had thought to rout. However, he protested, "This is no joke! You must stay—you must listen to me!"

"Fine, I'm listening . . . so long as you don't go on for more

174

than ten minutes! Actually, I won't pretend I wouldn't rather postpone the pleasure to another day, when there's less of a hurry. I don't suppose it's urgent! After all, my probable brother-in-law-to-be, we'll have the rest of our lives to plague each other! Didn't think of that when I helped you on the rings at school, did you? But back to business—let's fix a time to meet. How about Monday week at six, in—in the Rond-Point? I nearly said the Toc-Toc Bar. By the way, not a word about Tina to your sister, all right? I made a clean break, burned all my bridges, and now I'm bound for the estate of matrimony! Is it really four o'clock? I'm off!"

Desperately, Gérard took a step towards the door to bar his way. However, Vigneral had not actually moved; he was thoughtfully scratching his head.

"I tell you what, though," he remarked, "if I go off before you say whatever it is, I'll be a prey to uncertainty for a whole week! You don't know me—hypersensitive, that's what I am! So can you tell me in a few words just what it *was* you wanted to see me about, brother-in-law-to-be?"

Did he mean it, or was he still joking? What in the world could Gérard say? What could he do without making a fool of himself.

"Look, I can't explain standing here in the doorway!"

"Well, you can at least put me on the right track, then."

"No—besides, you're in no fit state to listen to me."

"I'm not leaving until you've reassured me!"

He was insisting now, still playing the fool, and Gérard, faltering miserably, simply wanted the whole scene to be over with as soon as possible.

"Come on, hurry up! I've only got a couple of minutes," Vigneral begged.

"Oh, go away!"

"No, no, you don't get rid of me that easily! You put people to a lot of trouble, you sow seeds of anxiety in their minds, and then you go wriggling out of it!"

"Will you please go away?"

"Fonsèque, what on earth is the matter? You look quite

175

pale," said Lequesne.

"I want him to go away!"

"So my brother-in-law will have none of me? This is the end! All is over! No—don't worry, I honestly don't see what could possibly prevent me from marrying Marie-Claude. Listen, send me a note about whatever it is. And remember our date: Monday week, at six. Lequesne, I hand my future brother-in-law over to you! Take good care of him! He's an odd sort, but I'm fond of him all the same! Five past four! It's not a taxi I need, it's a high speed rail car!"

The door closed on his loud and hearty laughter, the laughter of a healthy man. Leaning on the cold radiator in the hall, Gérard heard the clatter of his retreating footsteps as he ran downstairs. It was over. He had lost. He *was* lost. Why had he let Vigneral go? Why hadn't he stopped him, made a fuss? Why hadn't he rushed downstairs after him? He could not understand himself. So sudden a fall from grace, such a great gulf fixed between the creations of his imagination and their ability to figure in the real world. He felt humble, tired and sad. One more marriage, the last. One more husband, the last, to come between his sisters and himself. This was the end; there was no breach in the rampart now. He would be alone for ever.

"I don't think you ought to stay here, Fonsèque. Let's go out," said Lequesne. "I promise not to ask any questions."

He let his friend take him to a bar. Lequesne found a table and ordered drinks. Gérard absent-mindedly sipped Vichy water, while Lequesne talked about his life with the English family in London. He liked it there, got on well with his pupils, and was using his spare time exploring the city's museums and libraries. He was planning to write a book on Swift.

"Why did you go?" asked Gérard.

"Now look, I promised not to ask you any questions, so could you return the compliment? Anyway, you wouldn't understand if I did tell you. You've never felt a need to turn aside from a path you've chosen—you've never given up a

176

struggle because you suddenly felt it was pointless. One fights, one despairs. And then, suddenly, life is so simple, the heavens so tranquil, the remedy is pleasant and close to hand. You just wait, and the deepest of wounds will heal! It's no good resisting pain, you have to accept it, let it wash over you, pass through it and soak it up like a sponge. Nothing soothes grief faster than *not* trying to get over it. Listen, why not come and spend a few days with me in London after Marie-Claude's wedding? Your mother could come too. I'm planning to ask my own mother over in September."

"My mother is dead," said Gérard.

They stayed in the bar until quarter past seven. An old man with faded hair sat opposite them, his heavy cheeks hanging like udders on either side of his nose. A cigarette was jammed between his lips like a fistula in a sore. He looked grave.

"He's a columnist for *L'Aurige*," said Lequesne. "I often used to meet him in the Deux Magots. Pathetic sort of fellow really—a failed intellectual, sick and bitter . . ."

The man ordered more beer. The light was dimmed. Gérard was overcome by a sense of infinite desolation.

"Come on, my cases are in the left luggage office," said Lequesne.

The old man had produced a notebook, and was writing in it.

The station platform was swarming with people. Baggage carts linked together went by, carrying luggage. An engine came in under the glazed roof of the station with an apocalyptic noise. A shrill whistle pierced through the other sounds. It was hot. The air smelled of steam and coal. Little doors opened on a huge board, notices of arrivals and departures came and went on it, and the crowd raised their heads to look. Lequesne had reserved a seat. A fat, red-faced woman in purple was saying goodbye to an anaemic girl on the step up to his carriage.

"Take life as it comes, take money for what it's worth, take people for what they are—and thank you again for accompanying me."

A barrow passed, laden with books and newspapers.

"Adolphe!" somebody shouted. "It's over on the other platform!"

Lequesne got into his compartment. His face re-appeared at the corridor window. Gérard came closer. He was deafened and exhausted. He looked up at his friend's thin face, with its dark, calm, magnetic eyes. Lequesne's imminent departure lent him a sort of melancholy and enfranchised beauty; he was no longer of this city, of this life, he was already far away. Gérard could not think of anything to say. His friend was silent too. There was a movement in the crowd around them.

"Two more minutes!" cried the fat woman in purple.

Lequesne shook hands with his friend. "Believe me, Gérard," he said, "you can't grab what you want from life, you have to accept it."

And he smiled with extraordinary sweetness.

When the train started, Gérard felt a terrible wrenching sensation in his chest. He looked at the last of the carriages moving off, indifferent, squat and grey, with its little ladder drawn up into place and its glazed light.

The crowd was slowly making for the exit. The platform, so recently swarming with people, seemed vast and deserted. Orange peel and cigarette ends lay about the dusty asphalt.

An awareness of his solitude seized Gérard. There was nobody. Nobody with him, and when he went home there would be nobody there to welcome him. When he woke up tomorrow there would be nobody at his bedside. He left the station, and bought a paper.

The sky was a dusky blue, soft and weary. A light breeze blew dust about the streets. Gérard did not feel as if his body were a living thing. His legs carried him on, he knew not where. Sometimes a shop window showed him the reflection of his unshaven, sweating face. A woman took his arm.

"Want a nice time, darling?"

178

He walked faster, and hailed a taxi to get away from her.

He disturbed a couple embracing in one of the arcades in the Place des Vosges. The man raised his head. He was young; his mouth was smeared with red, looking like a wound, and he was breathing hard like a swimmer coming up for air. Gérard saw the ragged shape of a sleeping beggar leaning against one of the columns. Two Jews in frock coats left the square. Children were chasing each other and shouting. Suddenly there was deep silence, and then the shouting began again, shrill and discordant.

Papers had been slipped under the front door. Not letters, only circulars from big stores. The kind of mail an old maid gets, he thought.

The table was set for one in the dining room, which suddenly looked vast and pointlessly formal. A plate, a glass, a dish of cold meat formed a compact oasis at one end of the white, frozen desert of the tablecloth. The dull light of the ceiling lamp blurred outlines. The chairs were pushed back against the wall, their leather backs retaining the imprint of shoulders that had once rested there. It was like a ghostly meal, with every place still occupied. And so it was, too. Poor human larva that he was, he was on the very edge of the void. The room was not too large for all these absent people, the silence not too deep for all those unheard voices. He stared at the empty space opposite, where four faces used to look back at him, and memories came flooding in to heighten his distress. In dreamlike confusion, he conjured up his three sisters and his mother, looking at him, talking to him, thinking of no one but him. There were no other men in the apartment building, in the street, no other men anywhere. Nobody could take them away from him. Nobody could deprive him of them. And all they wanted was to serve and love him. A sad sweetness rose in his throat. How impossible, but how delightful! How far his dreams were from reality! What were his three sisters doing now? Not one of them was sorry for him, or understood him, or would renounce the shameful pleasures of the flesh for him. Even Marie-Claude,

179

the sweetest and most loving of the three, was sinking to the level of a brute beast along with the others.

He tried to visualize the appalling prospect of his future without Marie-Claude. A lifeless apartment. Meals eaten in solitude. Silence. Lequesne had told him to wait. Wait for what? He had a very clear conviction that nothing else *could* happen now. He remembered the fat old man in the bar. He might become like that himself, a shabby, ill-natured pen-pusher. He would cherish stunted hopes and pernickety grudges. He might get a newspaper column to write and then lose it. He would be a dabbler in the world of letters.

He poured himself some water. The carafe knocked against the glass and rang with a pure, clear sound which irritated him.

Silence returned, that muffled silence which soaked up the sound of all approaches to him, kept him there at the end of the world, was slowly killing him. He did not want to eat any more; he had no heart to eat at all. He pushed his plate away and got to his feet. Out in the corridor, he opened the doors of all the rooms one by one. He put all the lights on too. For a few moments, the apartment seemed to be inhabited. They were there! They would come round the corner of the corridor any minute. He would hear their voices and their laughter. "A coiled belt will make your waist look thicker, Luce . . ." But nothing human now disturbed the place where they had lived.

An awareness of his isolation broke over him again, with a sickening undertow. No one could suffer this distress for him, just as nobody could eat, drink, love or live for him. "You can't grab what you want from life, you have to accept it." What had Lequesne meant? How did you accept something you had never wanted?

He put out all the lights again in turn. It was as if he were re-creating an abyss of darkness and desolation behind him. He thought he was like a cemetery caretaker, going from tomb to tomb before returning to his own cottage at night and the oily shine of its windows. He went into his room. It must be nine o'clock. The window was open, and he could hear a dog barking in the distance. He saw his unfinished translation on the table. "Mrs Ploughman took the stopper out of the bottle in which she kept a decoction of colchicum seeds . . ."

It was the *dénouement* of a rather silly story. Mrs Ploughman's dose of poison did not kill her husband; instead, it induced vomiting, the doctor was called in, saved the victim and foiled the murderess. There were fifteen pages left to translate. Gérard sat down at his desk.

However, he did not write. He sat looking into space. And then, suddenly, he clapped a hand to his forehead. He could pretend to poison himself! Terrify his sisters! Bring them back to his bedside, remorseful, afraid, and full of sympathy. He would take a smaller dose than the one specified in the book, so as not to affect his heart too much. Then he would be ill all right, but not in the slightest real danger. He would happily pay for the recovery of Marie-Claude with a little liver trouble! For after this scare she would surely refuse to marry Vigneral. Her brother's gesture would show her how much grief she was causing him. She would be afraid that if she persisted in her engagement she would drive Gérard to make another desperate attempt. He knew her very well; he could do anything he liked with her by threatening suicide. Why hadn't he thought of that before?

How stupid of me, he thought.

He would have to get hold of the poison. Suddenly, he remembered that when he first went down with rheumatic fever they had treated it with colchicine tablets. He had taken two or three the first day, but then the doctor was called in, and had prescribed salicylate instead. Gérard still had the bottle of colchicine tablets. He would take eight instead of three; that should do the trick. He must calculate the day and time of the poisoning carefully, too, so that his sisters, given notice by letter, would be there in time to see him suffering. But these were only details.

In his mind, he was already composing a letter to Marie-

181

Claude. "By the time you read this . . ." He imagined the horror of all his three sisters as they hovered at his bedside, watching him writhing in pain, cursing them aloud and calling for death! He was possessed by frenzied elation, and could not help uttering a cry. Then he clapped his hands together, and tears suddenly sprang from his eyes.

"At last!" he faltered. "At last!" As if he had heard a woman's footstep in the apartment.

VIII

Gérard put an envelope on the bedside table, beside the bottle of colchicine tablets and the glass, which still contained a little mineral water. Then he lay down on his bed. He had had a bath that morning, splashed himself with eau de cologne, and tidied up his books and papers.

Now he was waiting, lying on his back and staring ahead of him, arms straight by his sides. There was a bitter taste in his mouth. Once or twice he thought he felt a vague pain in his stomach, but it soon went away. His head hurt a little, and that was all. I can't have taken enough, he thought. But he was afraid to increase the dose. He worked out that Luce, informed by express letter three hours ago, would be arriving any moment now. He had written to Elisabeth and Marie-Claude the day before, so his other two sisters might arrive early in the afternoon. The whole operation was worked out with the utmost precision, but if it were to succeed he must be genuinely ill, and so far he felt nothing. The English detective story had specified violent spasms, nausea and vomiting. "A sudden convulsion twisted him like a pine tree lashed by a gust of wind." Recollecting this sentence, he felt frightened.

"But I had to do it! There was nothing else I *could* do," he told himself, in an undertone.

He looked at his watch. Two hours now since he took the poison. According to the English novel, however, it was rather slow to take effect. A dose of five grams of the colchicum seed decoction did not work for three hours, and even then the hero of the story was not going to die of it. Gérard had only taken eight one-milligram tablets. That was on the cautious side—too cautious, maybe. He still had that bitter, dusty taste on his lips, and his mouth was burning. He stirred up hot and abundant saliva with his tongue.

He closed his eyes and opened them again, looking at the

183

soberly coloured backs of his books on the shelf opposite. He listened to the sounds of the Place des Vosges outside. This was the time of year when young American girls taking the Course of Applied Arts wandered through the arcades, beautiful and proud, eating big oranges stamped with purple marks. Luce must be on her way. So must Elisabeth and Marie-Claude. Was that a ring at the bell? No, only the sound of a child's bicycle bell ringing in the square. It struck him that he had sent the daily woman home and the front door was locked. He must unlock it, so that his sisters need not waste time getting the *concierge* to open it for them.

He got up, went into the hall and unlocked the door. Then, suddenly, he staggered against the wall. What was the matter? His throat was on fire. His head was heavy and painful, humming like a propeller. Slowly, he went back to bed. As he raised a leg to get in again, another pain struck him in the stomach. He cried out and collapsed on the bedclothes, desperate and shivering.

"Oh, my God," he muttered, "I think it's beginning . . ."

He was overcome by nausea, but he did not vomit. Cold, sticky sweat ran down his face. He poured himself some mineral water, and was frightened to hear the noise of his teeth chattering on the rim of the glass. He realized that he could not feel it in his hand, as if his fingers were numb and frozen. He stopped drinking. He was afraid to move at all now. "Marie-Claude! Luce! Elisabeth!" he called, feebly.

Why didn't they come? Wasn't he suffering enough? It was all their fault! Was some stupid delay going to prolong his torment? And suppose he'd made a mistake? Suppose he really *had* taken a fatal dose? Suppose nobody came at all?

The silence made his pain worse. He felt that a human presence would have given him some relief—a face, hands held out to him.

Suddenly he heard the front door slam, and steps came running down the corridor. He thought he would faint with joy.

"Luce! Luce, is that you?"

But contrary to his expections, Elisabeth and Marie-Claude came into his room. "Gérard!" cried Marie-Claude. Distraught, stammering, she leaned over him, flung her arms around him, kissed his face. "Where does it hurt? What did you take? When? Why?"

They were bombarding him with questions, and he was choking with pleasure at the sight of their loving alarm for him.

Elisabeth washed his face with a towel dipped in warm water. Marie-Claude took his pulse. There were expressions of delightful concern on their faces. Their fingers were shaking when they touched him, their voices faltered as they spoke. They were acting just as he had hoped!

"Plump up his pillows."

"Perhaps he should have a hot water bottle?"

"Speak to us, Gérard! Say something! Joseph's gone to fetch a doctor. Are you feeling all right?"

"I feel better," he groaned. And indeed, desite the pain, he did feel a sensation of infinite peace and sweetness.

Tellier soon arrived, accompanied by the doctor, with Luce and Paul Aucoc close behind them. The room was full of people now. Gérard, looking pale and shrunken, was bathed in sweat and breathing very fast, his eyes rolling. His fingers clutched the sheets. His lips parted slackly in a clown-like grimace.

"Keep calm, keep calm," Tellier kept on saying. He had adopted the virile and organizing manner he employed on important occasions. Paul Aucoc was fidgeting with the knot of his tie, while Luce scurried about the apartment in search of no one knew what.

The doctor picked up the bottle of colchicine on the bedside table. "How many of these tablets did you take?"

Gérard did not reply. Instead, he turned his face to the wall. If I say I only took eight he'll guess it was a trick and reassure my sisters, he thought. He did not want them reassured. Their distress helped him to bear the pain. He was still suffering just as badly, and the persistence of the pangs worried him. Ought

185

the symptoms to be so violent when he had taken such a small dose? He was very weak, and foaming at the mouth like a madman.

"It's all your fault—all your fault!" he moaned.

The doctor gave him a caffeine injection in the thigh, and he began to shriek, biting at his fists.

"Make some very strong coffee," said the doctor, "and then you must give him tannin in solution. I'll make out a prescription."

Gérard drank the coffee, and was overcome by vomiting. Apalling convulsions shook him. He thrashed about on the counterpane, which was stained with his vomit.

"It's not really serious, is it?" asked Luce.

The doctor took the three sisters out into the corridor. When they came back, their appalled faces alarmed Gérard.

"Why are they crying?" he asked the doctor. "What did you tell them? I want to know! They said five grams of the decoction in that book . . . so eight one-milligram tablets isn't anything much . . ."

He was in the grip of panic now.

"Nothing much . . . nothing much, was it?" he gasped, imploringly.

"My God! It makes all the difference whether it was in tablet or liquid form!" exclaimed Tellier, his knowledgeable eyes wide.

"It's not true, is it? I didn't mean to . . . What? What is it? Am I going to die? You daren't tell me! I don't believe it! Make me better! Save me!" He clutched the doctor's jacket, clasping and kissing the stranger's hairy hands. Suddenly he flung himself back again. "It's all their fault! They deserted me—they betrayed me! You see? You see? I have to commit suicide before they'll come to my bedside! Too busy, I suppose! They'd rather have brutes and scoundrels—rather have them than me! They go to bed with them, they laugh at me! What do they care for my sufferings if they can have their dirty little pleasure regularly? You don't know them. Worse than animals. It's all they can think of! It's all they live for!

186

They have to satisfy their hunger! Aucoc! Tellier! Vigneral! What are they doing in this room? What are they doing in my home? They've come to watch me die. I don't want their filthy faces round me—send them out! Send them away! I want to be alone with my sisters. My sisters, mine! I won't let anyone have them!"

The doctor signed to Joseph and Paul to leave the room, and this seemed to give Gérard some relief. He was suffocating. He repeated, hoarsely, "I've got you—got you now, you're here . . . near my bed . . . there . . . touch me, touch me . . . oh God, I feel so ill!"

He was bringing up blood. He raised his face, soiled with vomit at the chin, to their hands, to their dresses. He looked at them, breathing in their presence as tears streamed down the ruins of his face.

"Why did you leave me? Weren't you happy with me, all of you? Weren't you happy, Marie-Claude? Oh, if I could only get better!"

"Of course you'll get better, and we'll all live together . . ."

Marie-Claude muffled her sobs in a tiny handkerchief. Elisabeth, horrified, rigid and pale, sat beside her brother with a basin on her knees. Luce was stroking the sick man's wet hair and burning forehead with her long, well-manicured fingers. Her tears had wrecked her make-up; mascara had run from her lashes all over her eyelids, and her cheeks were smeared with lipstick.

"Do your face again!" whispered Gérard. "I want to see you looking beautiful."

He closed his eyes. He did not feel quite so ill now. He thought he had been transported back to that long-distant time when his sisters used to sit round his bed if he had a cold. They were close to him now, as they had been then, young, loving, sweetly scented. He knew what frocks they liked best, he knew what made them laugh. And they were all clustering around him. "You can't grab what you want from life, you have to accept it . . ." Life . . . life! It seemed to him that he had lived his life all wrong, and his sisters were living theirs all wrong too, and everything around and within them was all wrong. He wanted to tell them what he was thinking, but the words evaporated from his mind like mist. It's very important, though, he thought. He raised himself on his elbows.

Yet again a dreadful pain struck in his abdomen like lightning. His entrails were boiling. Agony filled his stomach, like a hand twisting it. He was thirsty, and panting. He dreamed that a vast female body, naked and heavy, was moving on him, crushing him, struggling with him. A thick soft tongue like a clod of clay came into his mouth and stayed there. They were throwing earth on his face. He was being buried alive. Like his mother. In the rain. Down between walls of mud with ends of roots sticking out of them.

"No, no!" he howled. "Do something! Water!"

He began vomiting again, a mixture of bile and blood. He was dripping with sweat. Convulsions alternately doubled him up and stretched him flat. His body arched several times, resting on head and heels. Then his temperature dropped, his pulse slowed, and he became very weak.

"It wasn't a very big overdose," said the doctor. "I've given him the classic antidotes, but one has to reckon with the patient's individual tolerance, and your brother's was not very high."

At eleven o'clock they had to put Marie-Claude to bed. She was worn out with grief and fatigue, and kept saying she was responsible for the tragedy, and she would never be able to make up for it all her life. She rose again in the middle of the night to go to Gérard's room, but at the sight of his transparent face with its dilated pupils and blue lips, she fainted away.

Next morning, all was calm. The sun shone in through the open window, and they could hear the fountains splashing in the Place des Vosges. Children were shouting. A peaceful smile relaxed the sufferer's face.

"What are you doing tomorrow Marie-Claude?" he murmured.

Then his head fell back on the pillow, and he did not say another word before the end. He died at four in the morning.

This family bereavement delayed the marriage of Vigneral and Marie-Claude by some months.